Swimming in It

by Patricia Wild

To Kayren
with admiration

Patricia

January 15, 2000

ISBN- 1-886388-13-X

Library of Congress in Publication Data

Wild, Patricia, 1944-
        Swimming in it / by Patricia Wild
p. cm.
ISBN 1-886388-13-x
I. Title
    PS3573.I4195S95
    813'.54-dc21   98-54717
                                                        CIP

The lyrics to, "Devoted to you' by Boudleaux Bryant is used with the kind permission of the copyright owner, House of Bryant Publications, P.O. Box 570, Nashville, TN 37738

Printed in the United States of America

10 9 8 7 6 5 4 3 2 1

Flower Valley Press
7851-C Beechcraft Ave.
Gaithersburg, MD 20879

ii

for David

And I went back into Nottinghamshire, and there the Lord shewed me that the natures of those things which were hurtful without were within, in the hearts and minds of wicked men. The natures of dogs, swine, vipers, of Sodom and Egypt, Pharaoh, Cain, Ishmael, Esau, etc. The natures of these I saw within, though people had been looking without. And I cried to the Lord, saying, "Why should I be thus, seeing I was never addicted to commit those evils?" And the Lord answered that it was needful I should have a sense of all conditions, how else should I speak to all conditions; and in this I saw the infinite love of God. I saw also that there was an ocean of darkness and death, but an infinite ocean of light and love, which flowed over the ocean of darkness. And in that also I saw the infinite love of God; and I had great openings.

George Fox, 1647

Chapter 1

"You've really done it this time, girl," he shouted as he slammed the door behind him and stomped down the stairs. Jewell listened to his heavy footsteps going down, down, down. A piece of lime-green playdough, pebble-sized, lay on the rug a few inches from her nose. "All I gotta do," she explained to herself, "is just lie here." Slowly, oh so slowly, she breathed in: yes, dust. The loops of carpet against her cheek, the smell of dust, these predictable, known things comforted her. She breathed deeper. No broken ribs. She knew something was hurt or broken; there always was. She also knew not to gauge the damage. Not now. A throbbing bruise, perhaps, purple-black, a piercing sting when soap touched a wound; sometime soon, she knew, her body would roughly inform her, scream: "Something's wrong."

"All I have to do," she told herself again, "is just lie here."

Hers was a soft voice, a Southern voice. Once he'd loved to listen to her, her gentle, soothing sounds, the way she'd smooth the edges of her words, though he never really listened to what she had to say. Once it was enough that grocery lists, accounts of her day, narratives of the evening's television listings were soft and gentle and slow.

A crinkly, rustling noise at the apartment door compelled Jewell to gingerly raise her head and look in that direction. Someone had slid a tan business envelope under the door. A sudden, piercing headache weighed Jewell back down. She lay there and cursed: She invoked darkness and damnation, volcanic eruptions, hurricanes, tornadoes and all manner of horrific natural disasters she could name, curses of biblical proportions, and pain, great pain. To curse well was an art form much revered by certain sectors of her homeland; not a soul in the whole wide world knew Jewell was one of the best.

She listened to the outside sounds: a chain link fence clanging open, School Street traffic, blue jays arguing in the tree beside her triple-decker, and, somewhere nearby, a baby crying. The smell of the old Portuguese man's cigar as he worked in his garden next door wafted up to her. Finally, when she was ready, Jewell slowly pulled herself upright and walked toward the envelope. It was one of those mail order return envelopes, the kind where you could put a sticker on the front showing whether or not you'd decided to buy whatever it was you were supposed to buy. Someone had crossed out all the writing with a red Magic Marker. Jewell pulled back the flap. Inside was the flap torn from another envelope, white this time. On it was written "78 Esperanza Place." What was this?

Just then the outside front door downstairs slammed shut. Quickly, Jewell slipped the chain into its groove, then waited. The footsteps came up one flight, stopped, then his key turned in the lock. The apartment door opened, then halted at its tether.

"Jewell?" It was a honeyed tone, husky and low. A coaxing, tender voice, much practiced.

"Jewell, sweetheart?"

Without giving herself time to think, Jewell ran to the bedroom, crammed whatever she could fit into her purse, dashed into the bathroom for her toothbrush and a few other randomly chosen toiletries, put on a pair of sandals, then, as quietly as she could, crept into the kitchen, opened the back door, and inched her way down the back hall stairs. She opened the back door, went on to her first floor neighbor's porch, climbed over the accordion gate across the porch stairway, then down the steps. There was no one in the back yard or in the driveway. Jewell knew she had a little time; he'd stand by the cracked door as long as it took to persuade her to let him in. It had always worked before.

Even so, she cautiously walked the length of the driveway, then crouched below the front porch railing. When it seemed as if it would be all right, she briskly made her way to the corner, rounded it, then headed down School Street to the bus stop.

The triple-decker she'd left behind sat on a quiet side street. Now she merged into the sidewalk flow of one of the city's most-traveled streets. She walked briskly down the hill past once-elegant Victorian homes now crowded by triple-deckers and three-story apartment buildings. Each dwelling was fronted by a tiny yard and enclosed by a chain link fence. Behind each fence flourished a variety of late-summer foliage: here, towering sunflowers; there, deep-scented roses. In this yard, privet hedges and ailanthus ran wild; there, a rose of Sharon tree, and seemingly everywhere, feathery

2

cosmos bloomed.

But Jewell was oblivious to it all. She didn't notice the weary mother, her screaming baby in a backpack, who crossed Jewell's path, nor the Japanese college student on rollerblades gliding by, nor the pack of young boys riding their bikes up and down School Street, enjoying their last precious days of freedom before school began; nor the two decrepit old men walking slowly down the street behind her, carefully making their way around dog shit and fast food wrappers. Everyone noticed her, however. Her bloodied nose, disheveled hair, hunted expression; certainly her tightly fitting tomato-red Chinese dress with its high collar, slit to her thigh. These set her off from the rest of the rush hour crowd.

She reached the corner and counted her money: five dollars and thirty-six cents. Every few seconds she'd look back up the street. "C'mon, c'mon, c'mon!" she prayed to an unseen bus. This corner would be the very first place he'd look.

To distract herself, Jewell focused on the flurry of activity across Somerville Avenue. Directly across from her lay a tiny cemetery, its crumbling stones often festooned with plastic bags and trash from the supermarket beside it. There stood the Pigeon Woman throwing bread crumbs over the cemetery's black wrought-iron fence. A crowd of pigeons was beginning to gather. The Pigeon Woman, a Somerville fixture, supported herself and her winged friends by rummaging through trash cans and in gutters for discarded tonic cans and returnable bottles. Permanently tanned, dressed summer and winter in a pair of Black Watch tartan Bermuda shorts, a charcoal grey blazer, and go-go boots, her brown hair cropped short, she was a woman of indeterminate age. "I wonder where she sleeps," thought Jewell dreamily. She imagined a sort of log cabin somewhere, maybe near the railroad tracks, a combination wigwam and cozy hut made from animal skins and wooden planks, heated by a fieldstone fireplace; herbs drying beneath a low, smoky ceiling, and furniture from an Army-Navy store.

Her reverie was suddenly interrupted. Something moved Jewell to look back up the street. He was there.

Even at this distance she could feel his rage. A river of cars flowed past her on Somerville Avenue. No bus in sight. Wildly, Jewell brushed past the group of Haitian women waiting with her

3

for the bus and into the first available doorway. A beauty salon.

"Help me. I…" Jewell shouted over the din of hair dryers and syrupy piped-in music. She looked behind her, then raised her hands, palms upward, in mute supplication. Customers and hairdressers, stunned, simply stared. "Hide me," Jewell begged.

One of the hairdressers, a young woman with cascading blonde curls, put down her blow dryer and gently took Jewell's arm. "C'mon," she said. Jewell followed her to the back of the salon, up a couple of steps, and into a tiny bathroom. "He won't find you here," the woman whispered, then returned to her customer.

Purposefully, Jewell kept her head down and studied the items surrounding the bathroom sink. She examined the cosmetics, the lotions and creams, the heft and shape of each hairbrush, the telltale hairs in each identifying its owner. This one, now, this expensive-looking wooden one with the metal bristles and the wisps of what appeared to be naturally blonde hair, this one belonged to her rescuer. Only after she'd spun stories for each hairbrush and carefully opened each bottle, jar, and tube and smelled each one did Jewell lift her eyes to the mirror before her.

The mirror reflected a woman of thirty with a face of angles and points slightly smoothed over by pale, translucent skin. A scattering of freckles bridged her nose. Her eyes were silver-green and large, held open as widely as a child's. Jewell's almost garishly full mouth was too large for her delicate face and gave her appearance a sensuality Jewell accentuated by painting her lips with bright, bright red lipstick. Thick, curly red hair, shoulder length, framed her face.

Jewell tore the gardenias out of her hair and threw them in the trash. She cleaned herself up, then sat on the toilet and waited.

"You all right in there?" called someone. Jewell opened the door.

"Yeah, I'm fine."

"We're closing up."

"Oh."

"You got someplace to go?"

"Yeah, sure, I can go to my sister's," Jewell lied. Slowly she walked through the shop. "Thank you," she managed to the three pretty women busily getting ready to go home.

4

"You look better," said her rescuer, who broke off fixing her own hair to study Jewell.

The tiny brunette looked up from her sweeping. "I didn't see nobody lookin' for you."

"Yeah," offered the raven-haired one, dumping curlers and combs into a drawer. "He musta gone the other way."

"Well," whispered Jewell, "thanks again." She opened the door to see an 87 bus just coming. She flagged it down and settled into a seat toward the back.

It was September 1. Moving Day. Somerville Avenue, always busy, was clogged with yellow rental trucks and vans. The 87 bus moved slowly through the heavy traffic, wove its way past double-parked vehicles. Jewell studied the city passing by. It's not so much that it's an ugly city, she reflected, but it's a city that doesn't appreciate itself. That most of its buildings are an eye-pleasing two or three stories high, or that streets like Somerville Avenue are of grand, boulevard-like proportions just begging to be tree-lined, or that most of its homes were built in a century when a well-turned banister, attractive moldings, and stained glass were standard. These aesthetics, these architectural wonders went unnoticed for the most part.

If the city were perched by the ocean, Jewell thought (and not for the first time), the city's handsome brick factories and Victorian dwellings would be celebrated, somehow. But Somerville lies, instead, between Boston and Cambridge, and therein lies the tale.

Two old ladies, probably sisters, probably Irish, white hair in tight old-lady perm curls, bright blue eyes, sat behind her. Either from deafness or to be heard over the bus engine, they shouted to each other.

"So what'd they serve?"

"Oh, it was a real gourmet affair. Brownies, Danish, you name it. Father Henry was there. He-"

"Here's our stop," screamed the first. The bus was passing the Porter Square shopping center. Jewell watched them carefully descend from the bus.

Take me with you.

She got off at the Davis Square T stop. For a moment she considered taking the Red Line into Boston but then thought better of it. She crossed College Avenue to the little park at the center of the square. Scattered between the real people populating the park were life-sized statues made of some kind of brownish stone, their faces inexplicably black. Jewell sat among them.

An old woman in a tattered, flowered sundress, her long grey hair pulled sharply off her face by a rubber band, had been eating an ice cream cone on a park bench near Jewell. When she finished her treat, the old woman slowly walked over to her and handed her a quarter. "Get yourself something to eat, honey," she said, pressing the sweaty coin into Jewell's hand. She smelled of urine and rotting teeth.

"But I…"

"I know, I know," crooned the old lady, then went on her way.

The rush hour bustle was beginning to die down. A few Tufts students and earnest young professionals strode past; everyone else seemed to have gone home for supper. As the shadows deepened, Jewell sat as still as the statues around her. A horror more terrifying than a raised fist approached: darkness. Much as she wanted, she knew she couldn't stay where she was. Very reluctantly, Jewell got up and walked toward the brightest lights she could see - a well-lit cafe, across Holland Street. Jewell darted across the street and went inside. Confused by the variety of choices of coffee, she stood at the counter, shoulders drooping, for what felt like a lifetime before she managed to ask for a hazelnut coffee and a corn muffin. She carried her purchases to one of the small, round tables by the window and sat down. Lovely, soothing music surrounded her, delicious coffee warmed her; for a moment Jewell breathed deeply and smiled.

And the young man at the next table smiled back.

"Did you see that film?" he asked.

"Excuse me?" whispered Jewell.

" 'Elvira Madigan.' They used this Mozart for the soundtrack." To Jewell, he sounded like a college professor, each syllable precisely spoken, the information delivered in an I-know-what's-good-for-you tone.

"I never saw it." She studied him and saw a man in his late twenties, with broad shoulders, good teeth, his light brown hair pulled back in a ponytail. He wore a pale yellow Oxford shirt,

6

unironed and carelessly rolled up to his elbows, and wrinkled khakis. His eyes were kind.

"Oh, you really should! It's a marvelous film." He pronounced the word "maavulus." "Made in the '60s. Reason I mention it, aside from this sweet, sweet music, is that you strongly resemble the young woman. You both have all that maavulus hair!" He sipped his coffee.

Jewell smiled. He picked up his coffee and his paperback and moved to her table; they introduced themselves. "Do I gather you hail from southern climes?" he asked.

"Yes. Virginia. Lynchburg, actually."

He frowned and his nostrils flared as if he'd just caught a whiff of something rank. "Isn't that where Jerry Falwell's from?"

Jewell nodded yes.

He launched into a diatribe on organized religion which Jewell didn't bother to follow, a monologue of half-baked notions and pretentious vocabulary, a hodge-podge of Marxist views and statistics, most of them erroneous and culled from magazine articles.

"Was it a sad movie?" she asked when, at last, he seemed to be running out of things to say.

"What?"

"That movie you were talking about. The one this music's from. It's so sad, somehow, and a little scary – there, that part, now, doesn't that part seem scary to you?"

He stared at her. Oh, God, she thought, I've done it again. Why do I do that? Why am I always making them mad at me? As if from a great distance she saw herself lying on the rug, the late afternoon sun low in the sky, warming her taut body.

He waited. They both knew it was her responsibility to smooth this ragged moment, to smile and flatter, to make the awkwardness go away. And Jewell was much practiced in this art.

So very practiced that a couple of nights later, when recounting his evening with Jewell to a friend, he wasn't even sure how he'd come to take her home. "She wasn't even my type," he reported, genuinely bewildered. "Too skinny."

"Weird," pronounced his friend.

What he didn't tell his friend was Jewell's genuine bewilderment when she found her back covered with dried blood, or how she'd insisted on keeping all the lights in his apartment blazing all night long, how spookily silent she'd been in his bed, or how she'd awoken screaming in the middle of the night and had to be held while she sobbed in his arms, and that she'd mysteriously disappeared at dawn.

"Very strange," they both agreed.

"C'mon," said his friend. "Clemens stinks tonight. Let's go home."

Chapter 2

It was not a lovely neighborhood. The houses seemed even more jumbled together, the tiny yards more unkempt, the traffic even noisier than the rest of Somerville. Jewell slowly – painfully slowly for she limped – made her way along a series of winding streets, stopping a number of times to ask directions from children who often shrank from her, taunted her. Her lovely hair was matted and now appeared an almost rust color, her skirt was stained, and she'd replaced her sandals with a pair of poorly fitting sneakers. Angry sores covered her bare legs. Jewell now wore a fringed leather jacket, very soiled, very greasy. It was fall; many houses sported cardboard skeletons and arching black cats on their windows and doors. A chilled breeze pushed dead leaves along the gutters. At last she found Esperanza Place. It proved to be a tiny cul-de-sac off Cross Street. On the corner of Cross and Esperanza stood a large, brick, Baptist church.

She rang the doorbell at number 78. The house was an imposing, boxy Victorian, with a mansard roof, its pale grey paint peeling, its filigree neglected. Number 78 dwarfed the tiny bungalows on this quiet dead-end street. Three ears of Indian corn hung from a tarnished brass doorknocker shaped like a pineapple; there was a peephole beside the knocker. Jewell could hear heavy footsteps coming down the stairs, then pausing behind the door. Jewell stared at the peephole, she licked her lips, she smiled, she stood up straight.

The door swung open. "What do you want?" asked a thick-necked young woman in a paint-smeared sweatshirt and sweatpants.

8

"Who is it, Dell?" asked a voice from behind the surly woman. An older woman came into the coat-filled vestibule. "It's all right. I'll take care of this," said the grey-haired woman soothingly. "Come in," she said to Jewell. "How did you find us?"

But Jewell remained on the porch. The husky one glared at her. "I'll be painting," she said. "Thank you, Dell," said the older woman. She had the deepest, bluest eyes Jewell had ever seen. They both watched Dell disappear at the end of a long corridor.

"How did you find us?" the woman asked again. From her bag Jewell pulled out the envelope flap with the address on it, now much torn and stained and smeared. The woman took the paper from Jewell and held the triangular piece for some time.

"I don't recognize the handwriting," she said after what felt to Jewell like an interminable pause, "but I do recognize the method. Was this slipped under your door?" she asked.

"Yes," said Jewell and, inexplicably, began to cry. There was something about the woman's eyes and voice that allowed tears. The woman smiled at Jewell; her eyes were filled with tears, too. "Your journey has already begun," she said, smiling.

"Say what?"

Again the woman waited for an inordinate amount of time before she finally spoke and when she did, her speech became practical, businesslike: "When did you last eat?"

"I'm okay," Jewell answered.

"But you need a place to stay."

"That's right."

"Well, you can stay here if you'd like." She tried to say this casually, off-handedly, but couldn't quite pull it off. She studied Jewell's face. "This must be very bewildering to you. You're probably wondering if I'm about to attack you or pump you full of drugs and – oh, I don't know, do all kinds of terrible things to you. At least I hope you're wondering that. I'm sure you'll remain on your guard for a long, long time." She stopped talking as if suddenly aware that she was still inside the house and that Jewell stood awkwardly on the porch.

"Let's sit out here, shall we?" The woman came outside, pulling the heavy door firmly behind her. "Oh, shit! I left my keys inside. Oh, well," she said, more to herself than to Jewell, "Dell can

9

let me in. Here," she said, gesturing to the top porch step. They both sat down. Jewell could smell the slight scent of sandalwood and also of bleach.

Jewell stared at her. She was a woman in her early fifties, of medium height, with long, thick, straight grey/white hair held off her face with tortoiseshell barrettes. A rainbow of smile lines accentuated her deep, intensely blue eyes fringed with thick, dark eyelashes. Her eyebrows were thick and black. She wore a navy blue turtleneck, jeans, several pieces of turquoise jewelry, but no makeup.

"How long ago did you find this?" she asked, nodding to the forlorn, tattered piece of paper.

But they both knew this query was not a question of Time. The grey-haired woman's question was really an acknowledgement of Desperation: What was it that drove you to seek out this place? Why is it you can't continue what you have been doing for God knows how long? What had you been willing to do that you can't or won't do any longer? Which particular degradation led you to us at last?

"Long enough," answered Jewell.

"Then you understand what we're about."

"I think so."

"There are so many questions for both of us. But they can wait. Why don't you..."

The door burst open. "Margaret! Phone call!" barked Dell.

"Please take a message," replied Margaret.

"Fuck you! I ain't your secretary," the young woman snapped and slammed the door.

"I'm going to have to take care of this," Margaret said calmly. "Will you be safe here?"

Jewell nodded.

"If you'd like to come in, just ring the bell." Margaret got up a little stiffly. "Damn," she muttered, then pushed the bell. After a longish wait, a young, pregnant black woman opened the door. "Oh, Tasha, thank you! I seem to have locked myself out." She turned back to Jewell. "There's a place for you here." She smiled and went inside.

Jewell remained on the top step. It felt good to have been given permission to sit on someone's porch. How many times these past weeks had she been chased away or asked rude questions. She watched a faded and gritty yellow ribbon tied to the porch banister across the street. It flapped in the breeze that came from Boston Harbor, bringing the smell of ocean and rotting things to Somerville. Jewell sat smelling the sea and her own unwashed body. She lifted her skirt to scrutinize a large, oozing sore on her outer thigh. "Just until this thing heals," she promised herself, then got up and rang the bell.

Dell opened the door. "Oh," she sneered. "The little waif. How nice."

Jewell grabbed Dell's arm. "Look," she hissed." I don't know you, you don't know me, but I can tell you right now, I do not appreciate your attitude. Lay off, you hear?" Dell, truly surprised at Jewell's strength, simply stared. Jewell tightened the pressure on Dell's arm. "You hear?" she repeated. Dell nodded, Jewell let go. A whiff of something burning wafted through the vestibule; a cry of dismay came from the back of the house, a radio from upstairs suddenly stopped playing. "Dinner!" shouted a female voice. "Such as it is," added someone else.

Tasha appeared at the end of the corridor. "Come wash up," she called to Jewell. "Are you hungry?"

"I reckon I am," admitted Jewell. She shot a withering look at Dell, then walked toward the back of the house.

After washing her hands and trying to do something with her hair in a tiny, old-fashioned powder room at the end of the corridor, Jewell entered the dining room. It was a stately room with a very high and ornate ceiling, a marble fireplace at one end, and dominated by a long, scarred oak table. The walls were covered with photographs of women. A fire had been laid but was drawing poorly, filling the room with smoke. Gathered around the table were five women.

"So you joined us," said Margaret, getting up from her chair and coming toward her. "Welcome." Jewell whispered her name to the others, then slumped into a chair beside Margaret. Dell sat directly across from Jewell; the two young women glared at each other with unmistakable hatred.

"We begin each meal with a moment of silence," explained Margaret, taking Jewell's hand. Tasha, who sat on Jewell's other

11

side, took her other hand. Tasha's hand was rough and cold, Jewell noted, while Margaret's was smooth and warm. Still wary, she stared at the others as they bowed their heads. There was a brief hush, then Tasha squeezed Jewell's hand. At the same moment, the others raised their heads and began eating and talking. The fire crackled cheerfully; the smoke cleared.

It was an appalling meal. The macaroni and cheese was overdone, the juice tasted watered-down, the salad limp and uninspired. Tasha, whose turn it had been to cook, received the group's complaints with a shrug: "I got other things on my mind," she said. Discouraged by this listless fare, Jewell furtively studied the women around her.

At the head of the table sat another grey-haired woman, more heavy-set than Margaret, who watched and listened to the interactions around her, head slightly cocked, eyes wise, amused, and ironical. She wore a rayon flowered blouse, slacks, with a pilly acrylic sweater across her hunched shoulders. She spoke with a smoker's voice and the broad-A accent of a native-born Somervillian. Her grey-framed glasses kept slipping down her nose; Florence pushed them up with her middle finger again and again.

To Florence's left sat a young woman who never stopped moving. Frighteningly thin, blonde, with heavy makeup around haunted brown eyes, she ate with quick, jerky gestures, often interrupting her meal to leap up from the table and pace furiously behind her chair. This was Shannon. The others ignored her.

At the other end of the table sat Nadine – a fat, lantern-jawed young woman with long, sleek, perfectly straight mink-brown hair – who couldn't seem to stop crying but could seem to gulp down her food with loud, smacking noises. There was a hint of Native American about her, something about the shape of her eyes. Abenaki, perhaps.

Jewell judged Tasha to be in her early twenties. She sat, preoccupied, eating slowly, saying nothing. Maybe four, five months pregnant, her coffee-colored skin appeared lit from within. A tiny sparkly stone graced her left nostril. She wore her long, straightened hair parted in the middle and pulled back into a braid pinned at the nape of her elegant neck.

The meal had almost finished when a heavy, frantic pounding

at the door began: "Shannon! Open the fuckin' doah! I know youah in theyah! Shannon!" a male voice screamed.

Shannon stood, sat, stood again. Like some entourage surrounding a member of the royalty, the other women gathered around Shannon, all but Jewell who sat, stupefied, and Florence, who went into the kitchen to call the police.

"I should-"

"Let the cops take care of this." They could hear Florence in the next room: "If there ain't a crewsah here in five minutes I'm callin' the mayah. {Pause} Don't you worry, I got his numbah. You got that? Five minutes!"

"He'll break the door down," wailed Shannon, sitting down again.

"That door's plenty strong," soothed Margaret.

"How did he find you?" asked Dell accusingly.

"We'll deal with that later," snapped Margaret. Shannon began trembling violently. Tasha tried to put her arms around Shannon but was pushed away. "Get her a blanket, Dell," Tasha ordered.

"Shannon's put us all in danger," Dell hissed as she left on her errand.

The pounding increased, became more wild and frantic. The shouts grew louder, the threats more and more horrifying.

"Listen!" said Tasha. Just discernible above the din could be heard a police siren. "Please be ours, please be ours, please be ours," prayed Nadine.

Margaret projected: "And the cops'll jump out of their cruiser, and they'll be all pumped up, and there'll be an ugly confrontation, and the cops'll manage to land a few blows, and he'll get hauled off-"

"Does he own a gun?" interrupted Florence. "I didn't think to ask."

"No," answered Shannon. "I don't think so."

Dell returned with the blanket which Tasha gently wrapped around the quivering young woman. The siren was very close now.

And the pounding and shouts stopped. The siren continued on its way up Cross Street. "Probably an ambulance," offered Florence. The group continued to stand around Shannon. Finally, they heard the screech of brakes, an authoritative knock at the front door. Florence went to answer. She led the cop into the dining room.

13

He was a tall man, over six feet, with broad shoulders and the slightest hint of a belly protruding over his belt. He stood with his weight resting firmly on his heels. His hat hid his hair, but his deep tan and Roman nose and dark eyes and eyebrows revealed Italian ancestry. His maleness in that room of women electrified the moment; they could feel it, so could he. Nadine stopped her incessant snuffling. In fact, she maneuvered to a position behind the officer who began asking Shannon a series of questions. "Nice buns," she mouthed to the group. Shannon snickered.

The cop filled out some kind of form, discussed a restraining order, then left. Each woman, in turn, went to the front door to make sure it was securely fastened; each checked the back door, as well. These rituals completed, Margaret blew out the dining room table candles, then spoke: "Let's pray about this, shall we?"

Oh, Lord, thought Jewell. I knew I was going to pay a heavy price for that sorry meal.

Still, she followed the others into a book-lined room. Shannon and Nadine plopped onto a sagging couch, Florence commandeered an arm chair, while the others sat in a kind of a circle on the floor, which was covered by a threadbare oriental. Jewell lowered herself beside Margaret. She studied the room. She was relieved to discover no bleeding Jesuses, no crosses, no blue-clad Marys praying dolefully to the skies, no shafts of light breaking through ominous clouds.

"We speak out of silence," instructed Margaret. "And we say what is in our hearts. When someone speaks, we take that in." And she cupped her hands, pulled them toward her stomach. "We allow the silence to speak to us, too."

Three hots and a cot, three hots and a cot, thought Jewell. The hell with my leg. I'm leavin' tomorrow.

The room became relatively quiet. Shannon and Nadine, still restless, finally found comfortable niches for themselves and settled into a kind of bored meditation. Tasha sat cross-legged, her palms held outward, her face in repose, eyes shut. Florence buried her head in her hands. Jewell watched Margaret's face unfold somehow: the tightness beside the grey-haired woman's eyes and mouth loosened, her breathing slowed.

It was Dell, sitting somewhat separately from the others, who broke the silence: "What good's a restraining order or if the cops

14

know what color his eyes are? He got away. But he'll be back. He'll hide somewhere and jump her. Or maybe one of us. Where'll the cops be then? Dunkin' Donuts, that's where. And she'll be dead."

No one said anything to this. At first, Jewell felt very uncomfortable. Hadn't they heard? Didn't anyone care? Were they all just going to sit there? Wasn't anyone going to say something? But as the minutes wore on and Dell's words hovered in the room, the anger and the fear she acknowledged took on a kind of dignity, and Jewell found herself focused on Dell but also feeling strangely connected to the others, as if they were all somehow inside each other's minds and thinking the same way together: Stuck. Caught. Trapped. Huddled, cowering together behind a sturdy door. Same old story, same old tale. There was a collective sigh and then: "I'm tired of being afraid," began Florence, raising her head to address the group. Her eyes flashed as she spoke. "I'm tired of reactin'. I wanna act. Maybe we get a big, mean-lookin' dog. Maybe we hire a bodyguard. Maybe we do Model Muggin'. I don't cayah. I spent my whole life holdin' my breath, waitin' for the next blow. I'm not waitin' another second."

There was a brief pause, then Tasha chimed in. "Maybe we do a Thelma and Louise. Blow him up!"

"Yeah!" agreed Nadine. But as the silence asserted itself again, Jewell sensed something wrong, although she had no clear idea what it might be. After some time Margaret spoke: "We've never had to deal with this before, this threat right at our doorstep. So it's no wonder we're contemplating the usual stuff. But we can't. We just can't," she repeated slowly, gazing around the room at each of them. "We can't allow ourselves to be victims, but we can't let ourselves become like them, either. Yes, we're angry, yes, we're afraid. But we can't allow ourselves to get caught up in the same old cycle."

Dell leapt to her feet. "You're crazy, you know that? You're losing it, Margaret, you really are. First, you let Little Orphan Annie stay here, no discussions, no questions – how do we know she's not using? Then you preach this nonviolent shit." Her eyes filled with tears.

Clumsily (perhaps a shade too clumsily? wondered Jewell), Margaret stood and very gently held the sobbing woman in her arms, then led Dell to the couch. A petulant Shannon moved over a little, just a little. Aware of the group's attention, Shannon blurted out: "Well, whataya lookin' at me for? I can't help it if he came here. I swear I didn't tell him where I was. I dunno how he found me. He did. That's all. He did. Look, he's the fatha of my kids, all right? Ya know what I'm sayin'? He's my kids' fatha!" And she stared at everyone defiantly.

Across the room Tasha glowed, Tasha burned, Tasha was on fire. But because she knew she was supposed to wait, she waited although it was clear she was ready now. She was just doing this little silence thing to please Margaret and Florence. When she thought she'd kept it bottled up long enough, Tasha uncorked: "My fatha used to come inta my room late at night when I was around ten and he'd start in on me. Touchin'. Feelin'. Makin' me do a whole lotta stuff I didn't wanna do. And all the time whisperin' trash." She looked squarely at Shannon. "So don't be sayin' 'fatha' like it's some kinda holy word or somethin'. My fatha was the devil."

"We're getting away from the-" Florence began but Margaret interrupted her. "No," she said forcefully. "We're getting to the heart of it. The core. The center." She looked over at Florence who sat as if struck by an open palm. "I'm sorry, Florence," she said more gently. "I'm breaking all the rules, here. Something's happening, though, and I think we should let it keep on going. Could we please try a little longer?" She looked around the room. "Please?"

Three hots and a cot and tomorrow I leave.

A nasty silence ensued, punctuated by Dell's snuffling. The cohesion was gone; each woman sat alone. Jewell counted books on the shelves, she studied the line of demarcation between Shannon's roots and her blonde hair, she tried to predict when Dell would sniff again (Now! Uh, no, a little too late). She watched Florence who again hid her face in her hands; is she really awake? She waited, prayed something would happen.

And then, finally: "I never wanted to tell anyone this, before," began Nadine, "but tonight it's almost like I have to. Like you're making me confess, Margaret. Which is whacked. Because I'm not the one. It was my stepfatha. And my mom. Even when I told her what was happening, she wouldn't believe me. So I ran away." Nadine gulped for air. "But like I said before, I always thought this was my dirty little secret. I never thought I'd tell anyone."

"Neither did I," I said.

Chapter 3

Believe me when I tell you: This is how I see the world. There are the hunted and there are the hunters. There are the preyed upon and there are those who prey. There are the broken and the ones who have broken them.

Here. Look hard at this. What do you see? This photo was in my wallet the night I left home. It's been with me ever since. For fifteen years. I was going to give it to my father; I never did. Every once in a while, I pull this picture out of whatever purse or bag I own at the time and really, really stare at it. Take a look. Pay close attention to the impossibly fussy dress, the elaborately curled hair, lipstick on those babylike lips, the rouged cheeks, the model pose. Is this a victim? No, you say. Of course not. It's a dog-eared, silly picture of some kid, maybe five, maybe six, with ridiculous hair and an ugly dress. But I am telling you different. This is a victim. This is me.

What I know, what I think I know; what I remember, what I think I remember. You might as well ask me to rattle off my times tables. Yeah, I've got the two's and the five's down pat. But there are gaps, great, gaping holes. Trust nothing of what I am about to relate.

My father left my mother when I was three. I believe I have two memories of him: When I was maybe two, two and a half, he, my mother, and I walked in the moonlight, they on either side of me, my arms raised high to hold their hands. We walked without speaking through trees along a gravel path. It was cold, I remember, and we walked slowly, a full moon lighting our way. Did the pebbles sparkle in the moonlight? I seem to remember that they did.

I can remember my daddy singing to me, too. I have a clear recollection of his tenor voice, the way he sang "Love Me Tender."

My father sang, still does, like he truly cared about how his voice sounded. He sang as if that mushy song were his own, not borrowed from Elvis. I'll never forget that.

Of course, I also think I can remember a bear, a genuine grizzly, ambling down Peakland Place near my grandmother's house. A

17

bear on his hind legs in Lynchburg, Virginia? But I can remember it clearly. And I can tell you this: Just a couple of years ago, on the Red Line, I caught just the briefest whiff of English Leather on another passenger; I think he got on at Harvard Square. But that smell brought back such a powerful memory I threw up all over myself.

When I was old enough to ask questions, my mother tried to convince me my father had died in Vietnam. One day, just before I left home for good, I took the bus downtown. I climbed up Monument Terrace, a long, long stairway up one of Lynchburg's seven hills. Ignoring all the statues and plaques and the noble hero crap from all the other wars, I climbed straight up those stairs without stopping until, breathless, I got about halfway up. There, near the little stone Unitarian church all the Yankees go to, was my destination: the Vietnam Memorial. Compared to all the flowery stuff I'd just passed, the memorial was pretty disappointing. Just a hunk of marble really, with some names on it. And, of course, my daddy's name wasn't among them. Just like I'd always known. It was springtime, I remember, a warm, gentle Virginian spring. The dogwoods were in full bloom, and I can remember flying up that staircase fully expecting my daddy to be standing in front of the church waiting for me. He wasn't.

My mother was a rageful, angry woman. I remember her slamming things: slamming down the iron, the thump it made, the steam hissing out, her hissing at me.

"You never. . ."

"Seems to me you ought to. . ."

"I go to all this trouble and you. . ." She slammed down the silverware, slammed down food, TV dinners mostly, she slammed on the brakes, drove as if the other drivers were united against her. Scrunched up against the passenger seat door, my body as far away as possible from hers, I'd silently watch her and wonder: Had she always been this way? Had she always been such a hateful person? Had my father's abandonment produced this lifelong rage? Or was this, somehow, my fault? Now, of course, I look back and wonder: Did my mother and I share the same shameful secret? Could that be why she was so angry?

Like Nancy Drew, I searched for clues: My mother's childhood photographs, carefully preserved by my grandmother, revealed a thoughtful child, often photographed with the tiniest crease between her lovely, dark eyes, a child who pondered the camera and the world around her with some concern, certainly, but, as far as I could tell, with hope and trust. I'd stare at her high school yearbook picture. There she sat, her lovely neck jutting out from a black sweater adorned with a slender strand of pearls, her wide, brown eyes forever soft, forever forgiving; pert, radiant, straight white teeth like a showgirl, smiling a million-dollar smile. Can you tell from her smile that she's already pregnant with me? A tiny me swimming around in her womb?

More clues: The stories my mother told me, stories about what life was like before, as she called them, Big Changes. These stories were my childhood fairy tales until I was old enough to read fairy tales in books for myself. "I felt like my whole life kept getting turned inside out," she'd say to me. Again and again I'd ask her to tell me about the times when women wore white gloves to go shopping. Or when the Tacky Yankees, hundreds of families, moved to sleepy Lynchburg. When the handsome, young Catholic from Massachusetts became president of the United States. What E.C. Glass High School was like before integration.

Once, I remember, I challenged her on her historical accuracy. "How can you call that 'integration'?" I asked. "I've looked at your yearbook a hundred times. And all I ever saw was one skinny, frightened black kid tucked away in a corner somewhere."

She looked at me like she always did: like she was contemplating hitting me hard. To my relief she merely shrugged her lovely shoulders. "All right," she admitted. "It was only a couple of negras but it was a Big Change, Jewell. I'm telling you. A Big Change."

You must understand that although she and I lived in a pokey, little house off Boonsboro Road, my mother had grown up in a spacious, peach-colored stucco house on Peakland Place. Her daddy managed Langhorne's, a four-story department store right on Main Street. (By the way, if you've never been to Lynchburg, the correct pronunciation is "Lang urns.") My grandfather ran The Store for its owners, the Gifford family, who reigned over Roanoke, Langhorne's, and my grandfather.

The Store. Now there was another Big Change. According to my mother, Langhorne's was the most elegant yet the friendliest place to shop in the whole world. Better than Bloomingdale's. "There was always a kind of a hush in The Store, even at Christmas," she'd tell me while savagely sticking pins into whatever garment she was working on. "You kinda slid your way into the place, and there was always that lovely sound of the fountain there on the first floor. I believe it was those thick carpets. But also because people respected the place…" And then she'd be off again about how lovely, how serene Lynchburg had been before the Tacky Yankees had ruined it. How she and her mother would be treated like royalty by the sales help at The Store. What gorgeous clothes she had. And on and on and on. The great irony is that my mother, this Southern princess with her three-piece sweater sets and tasseled loafers, her circle pins and her round-collared blouses, fell for one of those Tacky Yankees. Fell hard.

My father wore a beret. He had read Kerouac and Ginsburg. My daddy had green eyes and wrote poetry. I read some of it when I lived with him. He apparently stole his stuff from Ferlinghetti. But the Southern princess didn't know that. Accustomed as she was to either impeccably dressed prigs from nearby Virginia Episcopal School or sweaty football players, my mother was swept away by this seventeen year-old pseudo-beatnik with the sensitive eyes and the black turtleneck.

His name was Sean McCormick. "Kin to the Speaker of the House," my mother had claimed when she first introduced him to her appalled parents. He was a lithe, wiry young man, not much taller than my mother, with dark eyebrows, dark hair, dark beard and the white, white skin of the "Black Irish." My daddy ran the 880-relay and, remarkable for those early '60s times, did his own thing. He grew a beard when every other white male emulated the Beach Boys. He talked openly of his drug experiences – paltry experiences, really: he'd smoked marijuana twice at his older sister's "pad" in Greenwich Village. But my favorite story about my father was how he and my mother were the first couple at their high school to publicly dance that most taboo of dances – The Twist.

My own story is about gaps, about lies, about tight-lipped silences, and right in the middle of it all – a great, big, nasty, foul-smelling secret. But, for some reason, whenever I asked my mother to tell me The Twist story, she would do so with genuine delight.

E.C. Glass High School teenagers experienced an immediate and apparently profound reaction to the new dance from New York City's Peppermint Lounge. Usually, folks in Lynchburg were disdainful of anything coming out of New York. But this was different. This new dance, a dance in which partners didn't touch each other, awakened something. Or so my mother told me, again and again. All over town, from Fort Hill to Rivermont, my mother's classmates talked about and practiced The Twist. "You'd pretend you were drying your behind with a very big towel. That's how you'd do it, Jewell."

But, as she explained to me, Mr. Milam, the yardstick-wielding vice principal, considered The Twist obscene. He let it be known that anyone caught doing The Twist at the usual Friday night dance would be expelled.

Well. Because of my father's appearance and behavior, he'd been dismissed as being gay. Or "queer" as they said in those days. He couldn't possibly be normal now, could he?

"'Least that's what I thought," she'd say, the sewing machine whirring as she spoke. "But he came right up to me that night – we'd just played Roanoke, I remember, and we'd won – and he looked at me with those eyes of his and led me onto the dance floor. And then – I'll never forget this – he gave me this look as though he knew I'd been practicing in front of my mother's full-length mirror, just like he had, and that the two of us were just so ready – even though I'd never spoken to him before in my life – and we started twisting like we'd been doing this for months! And there's Mr. Milam. He's circling around us, watching us – everybody's watching us – but of course Sean's queer so what we're doing, well, it can't be wrong, now, can it!" And she'd chuckle, a throaty, rich sound I seldom got to hear. "Funny thing is, since we stood so far apart, The Twist was much less suggestive than some of the other stuff we did back then."

Funny thing is, by the time she was a senior, my mother and The Poet were doing some of that other stuff pretty regularly. Usually on the back seat of a red and white Bel Air; don't ask me how I know this. The timing could not have been worse. For, just at about the same time my mother discovered she was pregnant, her father's boss, Marshall Langhorne, blew his brains out in a motel outside of Charlottesville. This messy suicide and the messy newspaper articles that followed finally resulted in The Store's closing its doors for the last time in May of 1962.

My grandfather had always been a preoccupied, "nice to see you" with-a-pat-on-the-head-as-he's-striding-briskly-out-the-door kind of a man. He came home that night in May to his peach-colored house and rarely left it again. I can remember him – I truly can – pacing the length of the dining room while rubbing his hands and muttering, sometimes for hours at a time. My grandparents had a wonderful rose and plum oriental in that dark, paneled room; the rug's border was cream with grape leaf shapes all around it. I can remember my grandfather pacing on that border as if determined to stomp those woven leaves into nothingness.

My grandmother, a pigeon-shaped sort of woman, all tufted fore and aft, retreated to her sewing room. It was in this room, a second-floor nook off the master bedroom, chintz curtains, chintz upholstery, chintz everything, that my mother tearfully reported her news. "Now, Claire, don't do anything to upset your father," was all my grandmother could manage. So my parents drove to some pokey little town in North Carolina and were married by a justice of the peace. For an undisclosed sum, he even predated the marriage certificate by several months for the young couple.

My mother's parents would have nothing to do with her. So the young couple was forced to live with the McCormicks. All I know of my grandparents on my father's side is what my mother told me; I have never met them. "Tacky people, Jewell. Truly tacky. They owned every electrical gadget know to man. Electric toothbrushes. Electric knives. Electric can openers. I swear you'd think you'd have to be plugged in if you wanted to live there! And I sure didn't. Thank God, Sean's father was transferred to Huntsville, and I never had to see them again."

"Didn't they want to see me?"

"Oh, I think they sent you something when you were born. I can't remember." The sewing machine whirred a little slower. "Do you know they made us sleep in Sean's little brother's room? And it had Cowboys and Indians wallpaper! I swear! Horrible people.

"You know what else? She baked! We had pie or cake or some

other damned thing every night." And my mother would look down at her still-slender body as if she'd just this minute escaped from those Yankee monsters.

The young couple was determined to finish high school; this part of the story I was reminded of over and over again as my own high school career went from terrible to downright horrible. My mother endured ostracism, she endured morning sickness, she climbed three flights of stairs on swollen ankles to get to a beloved English class. Not allowed to wear maternity clothes to school, she adapted by wearing round-collared blouses and her skirts hiked up over her growing belly. After graduation, while her friends planned their coming-out parties or shopped for scatter rugs for their dorm rooms, my mother searched for a cheap apartment. My father looked for a job. By fall, her friends were off to Sweetbriar, William and Mary. My mother was learning how to sew maternity clothes, and my daddy was selling shoes for Coleman's, a shoe store on Main Street. He'd had to shave off his beard.

The rest of the story can be told fairly quickly. I was born, my parents struggled, they fought, he left her, my mother's parents relented and bought her a tiny, Cape Cod house off Boonsboro Road. They even furnished our house with dark, heavy, and, to my way of thinking, extremely ugly furniture, which had been left to my grandfather by his great aunt and had been sitting in storage for God knows how long. My bed, for example, was a Victorian mon- strosity made of varnished mahogany, with carved pineapples on top of the bed posts and, more interesting, mysterious tooth marks on the backboard.

And then, much to everyone's surprise, my mother found a way to support us. From sewing! Actually, this turn of events should not have been a surprise to anyone. Clothes had always been sex, chocolate, bourbon, and drugs all wrapped into one overpow- ering obsession for my mother. Very early on, I learned I could pla- cate my mother, soothe her, pull her from a dark, ugly mood sim- ply by asking her to describe a particular outfit. To listen to my mother describe her favorite cashmere sweater was a strangely sen- sual experience. And her passion soon became my own. What my mother had been wearing in those much-studied childhood photos became my new pastime. While other girls my age were dressing their Barbie dolls, I spent many hours in my grandmother's sewing room pouring over these pictures. Here she is, age three, astride a sullen pony, in a camel hair coat and leggings set, squinting her eyes against the sun. Age four: Claire wears a flowered two-piece bathing suit at Virginia Beach. Here she is going to the Episcopal Sunday school in, as my grandmother would say, a "cunning" plaid skirt and sweater with a matching plaid collar, a beret jauntily perched on her curls. And my favorites: my mother in an impressive series of prom dresses, stephanotis and tea roses on her wrist. She stood beside an array of bland young men; I found no such pictures of her with my father. In fact, the only pictures of my father I ever saw were in my mother's yearbook, his graduation picture and the track team photo.

By the time I was born, my mother's sewing skills had greatly improved. She'd made my entire layette, including the fake leopard skin bunting I wore to come home from the hospital. She'd altered clothing for my grandmother's friends who took pity on the struggling young mother. When I was still a baby, she began her own little business out of our house: selling and altering second-hand prom dresses and their dyed-to-match high heels to practical-minded Randolph Macon students.

This second business seems a particularly cruel thing for my mother to do to herself. After all, the young women who browsed through the racks of chiffon and taffeta and sequined marvels in our sunporch were her own age and, therefore, a daily reminder of what could have been. Her customers' careless remarks to one another while being fitted, conversations about their classes, instructors, weekends, dates: such idle remarks are painful for me now to contemplate. Looking back at it, I can only think that my mother enjoyed her rage and craved a steady supply of pain and injustice.

No, she never hit me. But I can remember thinking time and again: "This is it. This is when it changes." My eyes at the level of the ironing board, I'd watch that iron come down hard on the fabric and I'd say to myself: "I'm next. That's me lying there." Stranger still, somehow I knew my grandmother shared my fears. For despite a shell-shocked husband and a furious, teenaged mother for a daughter, my grandmother managed, as best she could, to keep her eye out for me. Whenever I stayed at my grandmother's house, she'd inspect my body for telltale bruises or welts as I got ready for bed. This she did in a furtive way. But I knew what she was about.

I loved my grandmother. I really did. I loved being with her. But after that first Sunday night with Mr. Allen, I refused to spend time with her any more. How could I let my grandmother watch me as I put on my nightie? A special nightie, the one I only wore at her house: lemon-yellow, sleeveless, very soft; rayon, probably. Wouldn't she see? Wouldn't she notice something different? A disgusting smell? A telltale bruise, perhaps? A hunched over way of carrying myself? "She's too old, now," my mother lamely explained; from time to time my mother tried to placate her parents.

But before all that, my mother, my grandmother, and I performed a very different kind of Sunday ritual: My grandmother was to sit in her tanklike Chrysler, the engine humming, her window cranked down, saying, over and over: "I just wish you'd come with us. Just once. I just wish you'd..." My mother's role was to stand by the car in her flannel robe, one arm resting on the car door, the other putting a lit cigarette to her lips, and to repeat: "We've been through this a hundred times; why do you do this? We've been..." My role, a very small and, typically, a silent one, was to sit in my Sunday best beside my grandmother, my stomach churning, and to pray for my stomachache to go away. Sunday after Sunday, my grandmother would give up. Her ladylike ways were no match for my mother's rage. Defeated, my grandmother ceremoniously put the car into gear and huffily drove up the street.

I can see myself in our family pew in that Episcopal church downtown, nestled close to my sweet-smelling grandmother, sucking a peppermint Life Saver, playing with my white gloves. Just above where we sat, I remember, was a stained-glass window donated by my great-grandfather. The brass plate beneath it said so. The window was of a beautiful angel, life-sized, in a pale blue robe and long, flowing, golden hair. She wore gold sandals, one foot placed in front of the other as if she were moving toward me. She held three Easter lilies in her right hand, her left hand stretched toward me although she wouldn't look at me but at the arched ceiling. And I believed that it was she who, every Sunday, lifted my pain.

Now it just makes me sad to think about that sentimental little girl. I think of her sitting there in the family pew, beautifully dressed, sheltered and warm, her relief to not hurt anymore, her grandmother beside her, and I think how hard it is for me to believe that that little girl was Jewell McCormick. Me. A thread has been snapped off. Broken.

Threads. Now there is a theme. I was about four when my mother began her children's clothing business. Again capitalizing on her still socially prominent parents, my mother offered a line of custom-made children's clothing of her own design to Lynchburg's elite. And I was her model.

How I hated the whole thing. How I dreaded the endless fussing and tugging at my hair, my ever-angry mother applying rouge and lipstick and, especially scary, mascara to my squirming face, the panic over ladders in my tights or smudged patent leather shoes, the anxiety when we arrived at someone's home: Would we be treated like servants or honored guests? Would we be asked to eat in the kitchen or invited to join the others? Which door would we be allowed to enter? And, of course, there was the incessant worrying over hems, the evenness of sleeves, if a dress or coat might need a last-minute pressing. Was there an errant straight pin waiting to stab me? Pull in your tummy! Stand up straight! Smile! For God's sake, smile! My mother's panic, her impatience before each and every show, knew no bounds.

I had always been a quiet, dreamy child. Or so I have been told. Now my fancy clothes required me to become positively sedate. When I started school, my mother used my daily outings to Miss Wiley's kindergarten class as yet another opportunity for self-promotion. Petticoats, gingham, lace on every collar, highly starched dresses, hand-smocked, of course; these hopelessly old-fashioned items were my mother's stock in trade.

And, for a mercifully short period of time, Lynchburg approved. I was a minor celebrity for a while; my picture often graced the women's section of the paper and my fellow kindergartners thought me special. They'd vie with one another to sit next to me, bring me delicacies at snacktime.

I look at that beat-up photo again. This Jewell, now, the one under all that makeup, this Jewell I know. I feel. I remember. For although she is still Before Mr. Allen, the BC and the AD of my life, still, there is something in that picture that feels like me.

Thankfully, this time in my life was short-lived. It was the late '60s by now. Everything changed. Drugs, sex, and rock and roll came to Lynchburg. I can remember walking to Pearson's Drug Store up the street from my house, just so I could watch the glassy-eyed teenagers in their dashikis and flowing muslin shirts sit at the lunch counter and spout marijuana-induced nonsense to one another. "Everything is everything!" a blond, long-haired freak shouted to his friends, one time. "Right on," they replied. But there I was, at age six, playing the role of passive Southern lady when this notion was being questioned and abandoned all over town. My clothes were laughed at. I became an outcast.

By the time I was in fourth grade, John F. Kennedy, Martin Luther King, and Robert Kennedy had been killed. The Lynchburg public schools had been integrated. For real, this time. Vietnam raged. College girls stopped wearing prom dresses. My mother's best customers abandoned their artfully tailored suits and dresses for flowing caftans. Women of all ages wore jeans. No one, it seemed, was interested in frilly dresses any more. Both of my mother's carefully tended businesses slacked off. She frantically searched for another way to bring in money.

Our house was built on the side of a fairly steep hill which allowed the basement to be exposed on three sides. With a loan from her parents, my mother converted our basement into a cozy, sun-filled apartment. And rented it to Mr. Allen.

I choose to believe that I had my suspicions about the man from the very beginning. I'd met him before; he went to my grandmother's church. Indeed, it was my grandmother, initially uncomfortable that her daughter was "taking in boarders," who had recommended Mr. Allen. To this day I cannot bear to repeat his first name.

I can see him sitting in our gloomy parlor the first time he came to our house, how he sat on the edge of one of our purple, plush, overstuffed armchairs, his smell of English Leather, the way he rubbed his pudgy thighs as he talked. Mr. Allen was a balding, middle-aged man who sported vest sweaters and Chinese slippers. He was the manager of a bookstore in the new mall.

We talked about books, he and I, during that first visit. He asked me about my favorites. And after he'd moved in, Mr. Allen began bringing books home for me: *The Little Princess*, *The Secret Garden*, *Anne of Green Gables*, Nancy Drew. Hardcover, too. "You shouldn't have," my mother murmured each time he'd hand me a new, delicious-smelling book. "You'll spoil the child."

At about this same time, my mother abandoned her seamstress business; the remaining gowns and prom dresses were given to charity. No longer would she run her hand lovingly over creamy, silky cloth. No longer would she tell me stories of chiffon and lace and the occasions she wore them. No more. Now, sturdy fabric, sensible fabric, fabric which would Stand Up, replaced the gingham and calico, the velvet and the satin on her work table. My mother took up upholstering. She took up slipcovers. And she began this new career in the same determined, competent way she did everything.

One Sunday night at about this same time, Mr. Allen offered to take care of me so my mother could "see a movie, have some fun." He'd made this offer many times before. This time, however, she took him up on it; I heard the conversation from my room.

I go back to that moment again and again. And I ask myself the same thing again and again. When I heard my mother say, "Well, I do think I'll drop in on my parents for a while. My father's not been doing too well lately," why didn't I throw a fit? Why didn't I just leap out of bed, run downstairs, and scream at my mother like she was going crazy? Why did I continue to just lie there happily eating a typical weekend meal, a package of Oreos, and reading *The Secret Garden* for the umpteenth time?

Maybe it's because whenever I read that book, I became engrossed in pretending that I was reading about myself. That I, Jewell McCormick, was really one of Dickon's sisters. That my real home was a bustling, cozy home by the moor filled with happy children and the smell of freshly baked bread. That my real mother was that warm and wise woman in the book; I absolutely worshipped Dickon's mother. My almost-actual belief was that I had somehow wandered off from that cottage. Someday my real and totally fictitious mother would notice I'd gone missing and would somehow just walk off the page and come to Virginia to claim me.

So there I was, happily reading in bed, already in my pajamas, although it was early evening, when he knocked at my door.

"Everything all right?" he asked, poking his head into my room. He had a very deep voice. My mother used to comment how nice it was to have a man's voice nearby.

"Yeah, sure," I mumbled.

Funny, the things you remember. I can clearly remember him standing at my doorway, staring at a pair of discarded pink cotton panties with a blue and yellow butterfly print which lay on the floor next to my bed. I can remember how embarrassed I was that he saw them. But for the life of me, I cannot remember how he managed to worm himself into my room or how he persuaded me to let him give me a backrub. He was very gentle, I remember. Very patient. Tenderly, carefully, he massaged my shoulder blades – I was on my stomach – my neck, my scalp. He whispered. About books. About Toad and Badger and Rat and my dearest, my favorite: Mole.

His man smell filled my room. Oh, it was delicious. Liquid. Languid. He softly stroked my ribs. I melted. He touched the small of my back. I froze.

So he began again, even more gently this time, more patient, slower. And all the while, he's still chatting away about Toad Hall, Rat's boat.

This time however, when he reached my lower back, I raised my ass ever so slightly toward his fingertips. Just a little. A yawning, stretching, arching kind of movement, very slight, instinctual, of course, and bewildering. We both froze this time. I was mortified by my body yet also mystified. What was that? What just happened?

But ol' Snake in the Grass knew. He stopped for a few moments and then he doubled his efforts. Or should I say halved. What had been slow before became absolutely glacial. The touching and the stroking and the caressing became so slow, so skilled, so light on my skin, I almost doubted his fingers were touching me. Bare skin. For by now, after what felt like hours since Mr. Allen had entered my room, his hands were under my pajamas.

Complicity. Yes. Slight. Yes. More than slight. A whisper. But it was that tiniest curving of my spine upon which so much rests. For these Sunday evenings to continue. Not every Sunday. Mr.

Allen was far too clever for that. And for the nasty little secret to became our secret. We would never tell, now, would we. Oh, no. Our special time. Just you and me.

Butterfly underpants, a twist of my backside, fingers on bare skin: these I remember. But then? The gaps begin. The holes. The vague sort of "I think, maybe, but I'm not sure..." Believe me when I tell you entire years disappear. I don't remember my grandfather's funeral. I can't remember the last time I saw my grandmother; I don't even know if she's still alive. Getting my period? I don't remember. Junior high? A blank. Friendships, sleepovers, birthday parties, a favorite Christmas present? Never happened. Like that first night at Esperanza Place, when the fireplace wasn't working right, a choking, grey smoke clouds my vision.

This is what I think I know: I know I stopped going to my grandmother's. And I know I stopped going to school with any regularity. It became routine for me to shout downstairs: "Ma! I've got a stomachache!" then lie in bed all day reading. I had a new favorite by now. Charles Dickens. All those miserable, miserable children! All those cozy family scenes at the end! My mother, who'd had to read *Great Expectations* in high school, decided, after a few feeble attempts to get me to get up, get dressed, and go to school, that what I was reading was educational and left me alone. At least, this is how I remember it.

When I was maybe thirteen, fourteen, Mr. Allen moved to Chattanooga. With him and his English Leather smell out of the house, I immediately paved the whole thing over, numbed myself to what had happened. If I did actually think about those Sunday nights, I convinced myself that nothing much had happened. Backrubs. Kid stuff. Harmless.

Memory doesn't work that way. I know that, too. Three years ago, while I was still living in New York, it all came back. Maybe it was a smell, a certain song on the radio. As my latest lover, drunk and clumsy, thrusted and pounded, I remembered everything: The heavy, rapid, frantic breathing in my ear. The terror. The absolute certainty that I was nothing, that my body was nothing, a piece of meat, maybe, something to be rubbed hard against, a convenient opening for this red, grotesque, dripping thing to be stuffed in and out of. Again and again and again until that final seizure, that final gasp. That's who I was.

That's who I've always been.

Chapter 4

A miracle: My father's voice! Sweet and clear on a scratchy LP. Even though he was just singing backup for some no-name band I could pick him out right away.

"That's my dad!" I cried to Jane, our new tenant, so excited I could hardly get the words out." There! Right there! That's my father!"

Like we did every Saturday, I was drinking mint tea while she played music she knew I'd never heard: Paul Robeson. Bessie Smith. Edith Piaf. Jane Thorton was a Yankee, a Barnard graduate, and taught English at the high school, her first teaching job. Very thin, intense, with long, thick hair she wore in a single braid to her ass, luminous eyes; Jane - she let me call her by her first name - was the first person I'd ever met who dressed exclusively in black. I haunted her sun-filled apartment like I had once haunted the library. I was fifteen.

How lovely, how odd, I thought. Is this how God works?

For right away I knew what I would do. My dad's band, called "Sadie," had put out one record with a small company in New York. A surreptitious phone call to this company produced a poorly typed, poorly replicated band schedule that I'd arranged to be mailed to Jane.

Such planning! Such anticipation! But at every step, I'd wait for the thunderbolt, the sign from above that I wasn't supposed to be doing this. For like those early Romans I had studied in Latin, I firmly believed in signs and omens. And so while I proceeded with my plans, I constantly watched my back.

Once, just before I left, I decided to play with my fate. I experimented. Painstakingly, I moved each and every item on my mother's dresser: her silver-backed comb and brush set, the silver-framed picture of me at about five wearing one of her most elaborate creations, a nearly empty bottle of Shalimar, and some hairpins. Each of her possessions I picked up, then carefully put down again in a very different position but in such a way so as not to be detected. Somehow, I believed that the entire universe had already been laid out, moment to moment, and that the willful yet benign act such as placing a comb at a 45-degree angle from its accompanying brush instead of, say, an 80-degree placement, would alter what was to happen to me in some profound way.

I was wrong.

When Jane handed me that envelope, her face betraying her confusion as to her role in my endeavor, I knew for certain what I was to do: After Christmas, I would take the money I'd been given for Christmas and my birthday as well as the cash gifts from my grandmother, go to New York, and find my father.

And I did. In early January, I got on a northbound train in the wee hours of the morning, having told my mother I was spending the night with a friend. As the train proceeded toward Washington and it became brighter outside, my fellow travelers began to awaken. Yet the car seemed oddly, mysteriously quiet. Full daylight revealed the horse farms of northern Virginia. And I discovered that I was in a railroad car full of deaf college students on their way back to Gallaudet College after Christmas vacation. No wonder the car was so quiet! With wonderful animation, they signed to one another, made little grunting noises from time to time, laughed. This chance encounter I had not anticipated, of course, and it set me to worrying: What kind of omen was this?

I went North. By the time the train left Philadelphia I had decided everything was going to be just fine. This belief sustained me through those first terrifying minutes when I came out of Penn Station into the sinus-aching cold and squalor and majesty of New York City. Trying to ignore the persistent "ssss" from what felt like armies of Spanish-speaking men just waiting for a fifteen-year-old girl to slouch past them, I took a cab to The Green Noodle on Bleecker Street where I knew my dad was playing that night.

This wasn't like climbing Monument Terrace. This was real. I was really going to see my father.

It was a Friday night, but The Green Noodle was half-empty. I sat down at one of those wire spool tables, real close to the band, and ordered a cappuccino because that's what I'd been planning to do for two whole months. I focused my attention on my father. And he saw me but didn't recognize me. Instead, he saw a pretty young thing with thick red hair who was obviously trying to get his attention. He came over to my table during a break and before I'd had a chance to say, "Hey. Dad, it's Jewell, your long-lost daughter!" he started hitting on me, I mean really heavy-duty coming on to me, his own child.

I got to say he looked good: still dressed all in black but his hair much longer now and with little flecks of grey in his beard and mustache. His eyes were still that magical emerald color, and his voice, well, now he used his voice, if you know what I mean. He listened to himself utter each and every syllable, and you could see him take note of what really resonated. In other words, my dad turned out to be an attractive, self-absorbed, and not all that bright kind of a guy.

So. After he got real embarrassed for coming on to his daughter, for crissakes, he reluctantly – and I mean very reluctantly – introduced me to the other members of the band. There was Ezra, whose show-off banjo playing I'd noticed on Jane's record, Hal the bass player, and the actual Sadie, the lead singer. Sadie was a blowsy blonde from Oklahoma in her mid-twenties, also all in black, heavy, heavy eye makeup, who, when introduced, gave my father a conspiratorial wink. His look back at her let me know he was already afraid I was going to cramp his style.

None of this was going like I'd planned. It took me about a minute and a half to realize that my dad's band was not a happening thing. That folk music in 1977 was not a happening thing. Somehow, living in Lynchburg, I'd thought my dad's kind of music would be viewed differently in The Big Apple. I was wrong. Dylan had sold out long ago, disco thrived, and bands like my dad's were regarded as quaint holdovers, dinosaurs. People came to The Green Noodle more as part of the tourist experience in Greenwich Village than to listen to the music. They talked during the most doleful pieces, argued loudly with the waitress about the prices, and generally set everyone's teeth on edge. The Green Noodle, I should explain, was Sadie's regular scene when not doing the college/folk festival tours. But, as I said, it was not a pleasant scene.

"Shouldn't we call your mom?" he asked as we crossed Bleecker Street that first night. It was late, but The City That Never Sleeps pulsed all around us. "Oh, no, please don't," I said, grabbing his arm. He never mentioned my mother again.

He let me stay with him that night. He had a studio apartment on Sullivan Street with wooden beams and a fireplace. After the bumpiness at our reunion, he made a big, big deal about my sleeping on his sofa bed; he slept on the floor. A couple of days later, however, after I'd read all my dad's Ray Bradbury books, I took up with Ezra and moved into his place. A somewhat larger place on Prince Street. It seemed like my dad hardly noticed I'd moved out.

I was not prepared for how profoundly New York terrorized me. It seemed like I could never get warm. Or feel at ease. When I moved in with Ezra, I got real bored staying indoors all day (he didn't have any good books), so finally I crept out into this bewildering city. Either I'd spend entire days sitting on a particular park bench in Washington Square or, if the weather was bad, I'd get on a train and find out where it would take me. Once I spent a week reading every, and I truly do mean every, label and explanation at the Museum of Natural History. But try as I might, I never seemed to get used to "ssss."

I should say that I found nothing strange in finding myself in Ezra's bed. Or, for that matter, in a series of beds of lanky musicians. I like musicians; it's always very clear with them: their music comes first. I started with folk, then moved onto rock, then jazz. Sometimes I made money: waitressing; as a roadie; one guy made drums; I helped him. Sometimes I simply changed the sheets. Never comfortable in The Big Apple, I moved to Boston a couple of guys after Ezra, then to Cambridge, recently to Somerville. I've been traded like a paperback, beaten, slapped around, abandoned in godforsaken places. I've been wooed and worshipped, had pieces dedicated to me, toured, traveled.

How I come to be here is a mystery. A pattern has been changed, some fundamental principle has somehow been altered. I don't know the rules; I don't even know what game I'm playing. All I know is that the world has become a very cold and a very frightening place.

Chapter 5

Dell's furiously vacuuming the oriental, Tasha's gone over to Broadway to get five dollars' worth of cut flowers, Shannon's in the kitchen, 'BCN blaring while she peels potatoes, and Nadine's supposed to be cleaning the carpeting on the stairs. She's in one of her moods, though, one of those times when all she can do is cry. I hear her snuffling, shuffling down the stairs, the sound her wooden brush makes as she slowly cleans each step. Because of my leg, which is taking its own sweet time to heal, I'm seated in the dining room polishing silver. Under protest, I might add. "But the tarnished stuff looks more like what this place is about!" I argue.

"Please, Jewell," sighs Florence. "Just do it."

Our sainted benefactor is coming this morning, and Esperanza Place is in an uproar.

Margaret and Florence have been trying not to appear anxious but have only succeeded in doing what women do so well: generate tension without actually acknowledging they're doing so. Those two wise old ladies keep telling us that unexpressed feelings have a way of asserting themselves, then they turn right around and pretend it's perfectly normal to be waxing and vacuuming in a kind of maniacal fashion as if trying to turn this place into something out of "House and Garden." For the past week, they've been correcting all of us for the slightest infraction. I swear, if it weren't so cold outside and my damned leg thing, I'd be out of here so fast it would make your head spin.

This place feels like home, today.

Lily Farnsworth arrives promptly at 10:00. She's an elderly version of Margaret: penetrating blue eyes, translucent skin (much more wrinkled, of course), simple haircut, natural fiber clothing, sturdy shoes. She's descended from an early Quaker family who fled to Nantucket back in the days when Quakers were being severely persecuted by the Boston Puritans. Makes you kind of wonder why we honor those early settlers who, the story goes, came here to escape religious persecution. And then they turn around and hang people who aren't just like them? Go figure. But I guess her ancestors had the last laugh because they managed to turn their forced relocation into something extremely profitable by making a bundle from whaling!

Isn't that the greatest hoot? Esperanza Place gets its money from the slaughtering of those sweet creatures Channel 2 and all the other Volvo-driving, Mozart-loving, politically correct types worship! Not

35

that the Farnsworths are into whaling any more, of course. Now they live on Brattle Street and do good works.

Lily Farnsworth went to Radcliffe, never married, and became involved in what used to be called "the settlement house movement." Which is to say (if you listen to Dell who, as the longest abiding resident here, is The Source), she spent years in Roxbury preaching what was politely called "family planning" (birth control to me, honey) and teaching folk songs to little black children.

Somewhere along the line, she became interested in women's issues and started this place a few years ago. She and a few of her rich Quaker friends and other members of her family pay for everything around here. Which means freedom from all kinds of bureaucracies. Which also means Margaret and Florence are free to use us as walking, talking guinea pigs for their latest experiments.

Dell's not totally clear on the details: "I think it started out being a place where battered women could stay for a few days. Y'know – give me shelter?" When I questioned Margaret she elaborated: "We were very naive when we first opened this place. We actually thought if we offered women and their children a place to stay for a while, a place where they could kind of catch their breath." She gives a self deprecating laugh. "Now we know a little bit more."

Quakers, I am coming to understand, worship above all else, a thing they call Process. How something evolves, how it develops, the slow, agonizingly slow way some decision is made as all of us chew, chew, chew on each thought; this is what is important, critical, essential.

"And each of you," Margaret continually reminds us, "brings something to this house. Who you are is incorporated into how this place is run."

So what does each of us bring, I wonder, as I halfheartedly polish a candlestick. Dell? That's easy. She's the dominant female. Like some kind of female drill sergeant of our hormones, she controls each of our bodies so that we now all menstruate when she does. Shannon? Looking at her frail body, watching her perpetual movement, listening to her talk about her children, she's a living, breathing testimony to how fragile it all is. Tasha? Her blossoming belly, the way she keeps to herself; Tasha's about inward life, life

36

within, but not in a spooky, scary way nor a distracted, depressed way. Tasha is about inner strength, I think. And Nadine, who's usually a mess, Nadine's the opposite.

Me? I'm just here until my leg heals.

"Really, Margaret." Lily Farnsworth's voice is surprisingly shrill and crusty; no wonder there was so much tension. "You really must do something about this rug." They're in The Name Changes by the Hour Room: Margaret calls it "The Centering Room" (Gimme a break!), Florence calls it "The Pahlah," and I call it "The How Much Longer Room." The other guests call it The Library. From the dining room I can hear every word.

"What's wrong with this rug?" Margaret sounds tired.

"Just look at it! It's ratty and shabby. It just won't do."

Margaret takes a long time to reply, a sure sign she's very angry. I simply cannot understand why these Quakers are so afraid to just fly off the handle like the rest of the world. Maybe they're afraid if they let a little bit out, some great smelly, spewing mass of craziness and rage and uncontrollable horror will come tumbling out.

"Perhaps if you saw the rug 'in context', Lily, you'd better understand why I'd like us to focus on other things besides interior decoration."

"Whatever do you mean: 'in context'? Speak plainly."

"We're to have a meeting for worship here in a few minutes. Like we always do when you visit. That's what I mean."

Oh, Lord. If this dour old lady is really shrill now, wait until she experiences our version of meeting for worship. Because I know we don't do it right. Like the way Shannon just goes on and on, just chatting away about nothing in particular, as if wandering through some gigantic mall with a Visa card in her pocket with an unlimited balance, or how Dell uses the word "fuck" twice in every sentence, or that Nadine is either crying or praying for something really stupid and trivial like "Please, God, please, let me lose fifteen pounds by next Tuesday." Tasha's the only one who's seemingly comfortable with the quiet. I just seethe and squirm. I really hate sitting there; I truly do.

"The idea is," Margaret gently reminds us as we settle in our places, "that Spirit is in all of us. Even you, Dell. (Dell scowls. It's a routine they have.) And since Spirit is within each of us, we need only listen. Be open to what is within you. Wait. Listen. We don't need priests or ministers or rabbis to interpret or mediate for us. We have the ability, all of us, to directly communicate with something greater than ourselves, something eternal. But we must be open. We must listen."

I have no idea what she means. But if I do know anything at all, it's how to please, how to accommodate. So I just nod my head.

Sure enough, our meeting for worship starts off just plain wrong from the get-go. First of all, Shannon begins talking about her psychopathic boyfriend again, right away, before any of us has a chance to get settled, even. After that terrifying night, she got a restraining order out on him. Last week, however, he got picked up on some drug-related charge and is presently cooling his heels in Billerica. Shannon's breathing a little easier these days. "I know I'm supposed to remembah that there's God in him, too, and that there's probably good reasons for him to be such a shit. You know, like maybe he was abused or somethin' when he was a little boy? But I gotta tell ya, I just wanna kill him." She says this in her flat, slightly nasal, normal tone of voice. "It's hard, ya know? Sitting here trying to think about good stuff? I swear to God, all I want to do is kill him."

One whitish eyebrow cocks.

Then, almost immediately, Tasha speaks up. "I can't get centered any more. Every time I try, all I can feel is the baby filling up my whole insides. It's like there's no room anymore for God or Spirit or Whatever. Just this thing that keeps pushing on my bladder and making me want to pee all the time. Not pray." She sighs deeply and shifts her body. We all just stare at her stomach for a while. Then Dell begins: "My fucking parents called again last night. I fucking can't believe it. We've been through this a hundred fucking times! They want me to come home. 'It's time to forgive,' they say.' Your brother's gone. He's getting the help he needs. You must forgive him. You have to put all of that behind you, now. Get on with your life. Why are you still living there?' And blah, blah, blah. Yeah, he's gone but what about me? I still wake up every fucking night screaming my fucking head off." (She does.) "What about me?"

Now both whitish eyebrows are knit.

"What about me, God?" Dell repeats. "Why am I the one who's being punished?"

Of course, Lily Farnsworth doesn't know Dell's history: the second child in what looked like the dream family – stockbroker father, pretty mother, the brick Tudor house in Newton, the summer place in Maine, etc. But let's move in a little closer, shall we? And what do we see? Ahah! Doesn't it seem the least bit odd that Pretty Mommy wears those great big ol' sunglasses so much? And just what is going on here? It seems that Big Brother, four years older than little Dell (already a terror on the field hockey and soccer fields), and as delicately built as she is sturdy, has somehow interpreted his maleness and his first-born stature to mean that he can play what he likes to call "The Game" with his little sister night after night.

And there was just enough corroboration, just enough clues and indicators and signs and omens in the world surrounding those children to indicate that what they both thought was his right really and truly was.

Right away, Nadine starts in again: "How can you forgive someone who rapes you? How can you?" She looks at all of us as if we might actually have some clue how to answer her. "When I sit here and pray, I keep thinking about 'Forgive them, Father, for they know not what they do.' Or Ghandi or Mother Theresa or somebody like that. Somebody really good, you know? That's what I end up thinking about. Trying to, at any rate." She wipes her nose on her sweatshirt sleeve. "And first of all, it was my father who raped me, so right away the words mess me up. And second of all, I'm just not that good. Not like Jesus or them others."

And without warning, my words tumble out: "I know what you're saying, Nadine. I most certainly do. I have the same problem. All I ever come away with from these meetings is: 'God! What a piece of shit I am!' "

My heart races. Dell. I look over at her. But I can't read her expression. Nor Margaret's.

A welcomed silence finally descends. It is as if all of us are held in the gaze of an unflinching camera, and no matter how much we want to, we cannot escape from the pain before us. We long to turn away, for the camera to lose interest in this scene being played out in this high-ceilinged room, the only sound being Nadine's sniffles. But the camera doesn't move. It records. It compels us to look at ourselves without blinking. Lily Farnsworth stares at us. She is beginning to catch on. Her disapproving look mutates as the silence deepens. She looks at us with horror as the pervasiveness of our situations begins to penetrate.

And then, something else takes hold. Now it is our turn to look at Lily Farnsworth's face with horror. For we are witnessing another transformation, perhaps predictable, and as dramatic as a hailstorm. Her face contorted, she abruptly reaches over to Margaret, squeezes her hand, then gets up and leaves the room. We hear the front door slam behind her.

Chapter 6

Tasha rolls into the kitchen. Her plaited hair, covered with pieces of white lint from her flannel pillowcase, makes her look like she's just braved a blizzard to come down for breakfast. Slowly she bends down to one of the cupboards, retrieves a cast iron skillet. "Someone's left their mess in this pan again," she says, disgusted. She waddles to the sink and slowly, deliberately, begins to clean the skillet. The way she stares out the window over the sink, hums to herself, lets us know to leave her alone.

Nadine and I clink our spoons against the sides of our cereal bowls. It's a cheerful sound; we allow it to fill the kitchen. Dell has barricaded herself behind today's Globe. "Get this!" she indignantly reads aloud, "That fucking priest is 'remorseful.' Remorseful! He abused all those little kids, his own children, too, probably, and. . ." she slams the paper down, grabs Nadine's and my now empty bowls, stomps over to the dishwasher, and starts loading it.

"Is there any more coffee?" Margaret asks as she comes through the door. She's a real caffeine fiend. Margaret displays infinite patience at our transgressions, but woe to the woman who poured herself the last cup and failed to brew a fresh pot.

"How's Florence doin'?" asks Nadine. Florence has been out sick, now, for over a week. The flu.

"Better," says Margaret, pouring skim milk into her coffee mug. "She'll be back in a couple of days."

"Anyone want any eggs?" asks Tasha. It is only then as we look at her that we collectively realize: Shannon's not here. We don't need to check her room; the absence of her constant din, a radio blaring somewhere in the house, her continual pacing, upheavals of furniture in her room, angry, tearful conversations on the phone; it is this lack of noise which reverberates throughout the house.

But like the code of behavior among the animals in *The Wind in the Willows*, no one says: "Shannon's bolted." Women come and go here. And given how hard it is to stay sober, stay clean, stay manless, stay away from the lure and the terror of the streets (after all, for many of us, terror feels normal), it's just easier not to mention that one of us has gone.

After breakfast, I bundle up and go out to Esperanza Place's tiny back yard. It's a city kind of space, walled on the left side by the Baptist church; the back and right sides are marked by a sagging, weathered, stockade fence. Last night's rain turned to snow towards dawn; there's a light dusting of snow everywhere. The sun is out this morning and, standing in the lee of the church's brick wall, I am almost warm. A squirrel scolds me from somewhere in a neighbor's tree. I walk over to the birdfeeder cut from a plastic bleach bottle suspended from the clothes line. As I fill it with sunflower seeds, I think about the ghosts of Esperanza Place.

Their faces stare down at us in the dining room. Some woman made this tacky birdfeeder. Everywhere, I see mute reminders of all the women who have lived here before. Up to this morning, I could keep these ghosts at a distance. But now I'm compelled to think about Shannon, wondering if she's all right. Wondering, yes. But also, I'm realizing as I stomp the frozen puddle beneath my feet, smash the shards into tinier and tinier pieces, I'm angry at Shannon. How can she be falling for that same old bull? How can she be telling herself that same old lie: "He's different, now. He's changed. This time will be different. This time it really is going to work." The ice shards are now like powder.

I think of Shannon's story as I stomp. It's a classic. Sometimes, when I'm in one of my more dreamy, heavily-influenced-by-children's-books moods, I think of Shannon's family and all the other petty criminals from Charlestown as legitimate descendents of pirates and rogues. And that all of them, modern-day swashbucklers, chose to settle in Charlestown near the sea once plundered by their ancestors. Which makes Shannon a kind of pirate princess.

And which is also to say that the real story, the one about Shannon's father sexually abusing her when she was ten, and how she started smoking weed at twelve, met "the fatha" of her kids when she was fifteen, had her first baby a year later, how "The Neanderthal" beat her and the kids up on a regular basis so that eventually they were taken away from her, how she landed on the streets and finally found Esperanza Place; that story is much more difficult for me to tell myself.

All the telltale signs seem to point to the fact that Shannon has reunited with The Neaderthal. All her makeup's gone and her nicest clothes. And there was just the faintest whiff, like perfume on an ancient handkerchief, of aftershave in the vestibule.

Keep safe, Pirate Princess, I whisper.

A chickadee perches on the fence, interrupts my thoughts. He cocks his black capped head: "Aren't you done, yet? I'm hungry." Dell claims they'll eat out of your hand, but Dell's a liar.

I remember MX furiously barking late last night. Perhaps that was when Shannon made her escape. MX is our huge, stupid, very imposing-looking Black Lab/ German Shepherd mix. Florence got him after that door-pounding incident. His fierce bark resonates in such a way as to let all of us sleep a little bit better these days. He roars in a truly terrifying fashion not only at the doorbell and all passersby, but also at squirrels on telephone wires and neighborhood cats. Last night I'd assumed he'd been letting us know that the neighborhood stray, a pathetic Irish setter whose ribs show, was on a midnight ramble. I'd been lying in my bed under the eaves, listening to the rain, feeling the house shudder in the wind, the windows rattling in their panes, and remembering the times I'd been on the streets on nights like this.

If Shannon's disappearance weren't enough, apparently the situation with our sainted benefactor has worsened. "She doesn't answer my calls!" I happened to have overheard Margaret say to Florence on the phone just now. There were already signs of a deepening estrangement. A kind of miserliness has taken hold. Florence and Margaret are spending a lot of time these days turning off lights seemingly the moment anyone leaves the room, and they continually check the thermostat to make sure none of us has tried sneaking it up a degree or two. It's not that Lily Farnsworth isn't paying our bills; she continues to support us financially. It's just that the staff seems just plain scared to do anything that will further provoke her ire.

And so, meeting for worship is a bumpy affair this morning. We depend on Margaret to set the tone for our worship; her distractedness unsettles us all.

After much sighing and wriggling and an angry diatribe from Dell on the subject of Men and how every single one of them is lower than a worm, we sit, bored, restless, anxious for this meaningless exercise to end.

And I'm suddenly aware of how tired I am. Fatigue weighs me down; my shoulders slump like some ol' bag lady's. It's as if every muscle in my body refuses to work. I loll, I droop, I wilt. When, mercifully, we can leave, I can barely walk. Slowly, painfully, I drag myself up two flight of stairs and collapse into my bed.

Chapter 7

Afterwards, they told me it had been the flu. Feverishly, I laid in my narrow bed, a kind of Princess and the Pea in reverse, as more and more quilts and blankets were heaped upon me, and I slept and I slept and I slept. Only in the sketchiest way was I aware of things: the ancient radiator clanking and wheezing in the corner; various members of the house – even Dell! – bringing me ginger ale, orange juice, aspirin; the wind outside.

One night, I remember, the house completely quiet, I awoke to find a full moon lighting my room. And like a gift from the goddess Diana, a memory came to me as I lay in my virginal bed. I remembered – how was this possible? – my parents singing an old Everly Brothers tune called "Devoted To You." A corny, sentimental thing, but, like all Everly Brothers material, perfect for two harmonizing voices. And I could clearly hear each of them; my mother's soprano, quivery yet sweet, my father's confident tenor as they promised "I'll never hurt you, I'll never lie, I'll never be untrue. I'll never give you reason to cry, I'd be unhappy if you were blue-oo..." Helpless as a baby I lay in my bed, tears wetting my cheeks, my sweaty pillow, falling into my ears. Incandescent tears. They glowed in the moonlight like crystals. Tears of gratitude for this miraculous gift, this memory of a man and woman who, long ago, thought they loved one another. Tears of inescapable sadness for all of us – for my mother; for Shannon, wherever she is; yes, even for some of those lanky-legged men I have left behind; tears for those who have loved and been betrayed. I cried until I couldn't anymore, and then I slept again.

I slept through Thanksgiving. When I finally creep down the stairs the following Monday, hungry, shaky on my pegs, the whole world has changed. Yes. Really. Sitting in the living room rocking chair is a very smug and content Tasha nursing an oddly colored, wrinkly creature.

"What'd you name him?" I ask after making what I pray are the appropriate cooing, appreciative noises. I like Tasha; I really do. But the idea of children gives me a rash.

"Jordan." She gives me a beatific smile. "After Michael Jordan." When it sounds as if she's getting ready to launch into a recitation of the entire birth experience – "Dell was wonderful!" – I hightail it out of there.

But, it would seem that even more remarkable than the presence of this new, little person is the transformation of the entire house. The mirror in the front hall has sprouted greens. Little figurines of snowmen and angels and shepherds appear on the mantelpiece in the dining room. Everywhere I look, I see Cute! It is as if we are suddenly living in some pale, pale replication of a Currier and Ives print. No! Not Currier and Ives, exactly. Something from another century, possibly; something cloying, something unreal, something downright spooky.

The Christmas season is upon us.

And the donations! Brownies, sugar cookies, baked goods, fudge, hand-me-down clothing freshly laundered, mysterious packages whisked away to Margaret's office; every day someone from Esperanza Place drives to the Cambridge meetinghouse to bring back donations to our shelter. Boxes and boxes, many with handwritten notes expressing love and concern.

"When discouraged, do you remember that Jesus said, 'Peace is my parting gift to you, my own peace, such the world cannot

give. Set your troubled hearts at rest, and banish your fears.' "
These words, written with spidery letters, are pinned to a creamy
Irish knit cardigan I claim for my own. I throw the note away.

It is as if great forces in the universe have conspired together
to attempt to distract all of us from realizing that we're living in a
shelter and it's Christmas.

But, of course, it doesn't work. No matter how adorably this
house has been decorated, no matter how many butter-laden good-
ies fill the pantry, we know the score.

There is another factor at play here. Curiously, it is I, of all people, who names this phenomenon. And at a meeting for worship, no
less! "...so of course everybody's drunk by the time dinner is ready.
Nobody eats much of anything after all that work, then they all go
off to watch some dumbass thing on TV. So I..." Nadine's whining
again about yet another miserable family gathering.

Dismal times under individual roofs; this has been the theme
for meeting for worship since I've rejoined the living. Family cele-
brations gone awry, fights, tears, confrontations, painful moments
when drunken family members said what was really on their minds,
that empty, empty feeling when you were told you were having a
good time – "Isn't this fun?!"- and you knew you were miserable.

But something is happening in the telling of these stories.
Something inexplicable. I don't understand it.

"...so then my mother comes back into the kitchen..." All I
know is that I'm supposed to listen to this winter's tale. Somehow,
my listening, my attentiveness, means something.

For reasons I can't explain I start humming "Amazing Grace".
Margaret joins in: "...how sweet the sound..." And we finish more
or less on the same note which we hold for a few moments. We
smile at one another. The silence of this moment is delicious. And
I am encouraged to continue: "It's like we're all trying to live in a
'Waltons' episode, and since we're not, everything sucks.
Especially, now. There's this expectation that we're supposed to
meet about family and holidays and happy memories, and I'll bet
no one, not one single person, has a family or happy memories that
even come close to this, this ideal we're all supposed to have experienced. So they play "Little Drummer Boy" about one million
times to completely numb you out. Then they try to trick you into

believing that you're the only person on this entire planet who didn't share in this great, giant, wondrous thing. It's a hoax! The 'Waltons' hoax!"

So now it is my words that hang in the air. It is my words that fill this room. It is my words that I feel being pulled inside the slumped bodies around me.

But, of course, this Aha! must be countered, somehow. After meeting, Dell starts in: "So what are you giving Tasha's baby for Christmas, Jewell-Girl?" We're at lunch; her mouth is full and she has a spot of mayonnaise on her chin, so I do not deign to answer immediately.

"Well, now, Dell-Bob," I drawl as slowly as I can, "my funds are a mite low these days. I guess I need to get a job."

"Just don't bring your trade here," she snaps.

Nothing's changed. Since the very first day, this bitch's been on my case.

"Dell-Bob," I reply in what I know is my most annoying Southern and ladylike tones, "you and I are both here by the grace of these good Quaker ladies. And since our hostesses abhor violence in any form, I believe it would only be good manners to respect their beliefs. And while we're on the subject, there's something else I'd like to say. I believe that verbal attacks and, I might add, your excessive use of the word 'fuck' are a form of violence. So shut up!"

Bullseye! Quivering from rage, she stomps off to her room where I know for a fact she'll furiously write in her journal for an hour or so, then call her therapist for an emergency session.

Margaret is looking at me with Bambi-eyed reproach. "Come to my office after lunch," Margaret says to me.

Margaret's office is in one of the front rooms on the first floor. Filled with plants and books and photographs of women who have stayed here, her desk shoved into an out-of-the-way corner, and with a fireplace with two cozy wing chairs on either side, the space feels more like a parlor than the lair of a bureaucrat. A big ol' oak wall clock, a Regulator, ticks slowly and calmly. It almost never feels like going to the principal's office to come here.

Except right now.

After the briefest of chats (one of the things I find hard to get used to is the way people in the North just kind of barge ahead in conversations; folks just don't seem to know how to ease their way into what it is they really want to be talking about), she begins: "I was very impressed by the way you began setting limits with Dell at lunch. I think it's important for her to realize how her language affects you."

"Thank you."

"You might want to be thinking about how to set limits without putting the other person on the defensive. It's awfully hard, I grant you. But you see what's happened, now, with Dell. She's angry with you and she's going to come back at you like a ton of bricks. I'd watch my back for a while, if I were you." She looks at me with those gentle eyes. "But I don't need to be telling you that, do I. You manage to land on your feet pretty well."

"I reckon."

"This needs to feel like a safe place. For all of us. Would you keep that in mind?"

I nod my head.

"Well, I wanted to take you up on that idea you put forth at lunch. About a job. One of the members of Meeting, an elderly woman who works in the clothing room, noticed how carefully you drove the other day. When you picked up donations?"

I grin at her. "It would be hard to do anything else there, Margaret. They're all standing around looking at you anyway, and then there's the fact that it's a pretty tight squeeze getting past that portico thing. Of course I'm careful."

"Well, this woman is looking for someone to read to her and drive her places. Would you be interested?"

In my mind's eye I see me driving through Powderhouse Rotary and – Whomp! Suddenly, some asshole driver tries to cut me off! I scream at him, and the sweet little Quaker lady sitting beside me clutches her seatbelt.

"Naw. I don't think so."

"I understand." She pauses. "There's something else I think you should be working on."

"And what would that be?" I ask warily.

"Getting your GED," she says briskly. A tad too briskly. Now my heart begins to race.

"What?"

"Your high school equivalency."

Is this woman crazy?

"Do you know how long it's been since I was in school?" I ask indignantly. "Dell's right! You are losing it. Fuck you, Margaret."

I leap out of my chair. But Margaret jumps up, comes after me as I start for the stairs.

"Do you know how hard it's going to be to support yourself without some kind of training? Do you know most training programs require a GED?" She pants out the words as she's coming after me.

I'm on the stairs. I'm bookin'. Dimly I realize that my leg must be okay, now.

"I can always waitress. Don't need a degree for that." I shout over my shoulder. At the top of the stairs, I sprint to my room and slam the door.

"Jewell, the minute you put yourself back in that environment, you're going to end up doing what you've always done to survive." I can hear her heavy breathing; she can barely manage to talk. I think she's sitting on the floor in front of my door. She sounds exhausted.

I gotta get out of here.

"Leave me alone!" I scream. And after a few moments, she slowly walks down the stairs again. When I'm certain she's in her office, I grab my hat and coat, sneak into Florence's office, and take twenty dollars from petty cash.

And I am out the door. Hello, Somerville.

Has it always been this noisy?

An arctic wind blows down Winter Hill. It's one of those dismal, grey days in December, the kind of a day that convinces you that it'll always be sunless, always be bitter cold, always feel like death. I scrunch myself tighter and tighter against the north wind; I shrink into myself.

Cautiously I cross the McGrath Highway with the light. The windows of the Dunkin' Donuts at the corner are fogged; the smells of coffee and cigarettes and men inside are dizzying. Like some stumblebum drunk, I stagger back outside. Somehow the exhaust fumes from the highway sober me as I walk up Prospect Hill.

At the base of the hill's tower, a castlelike two story stone structure commemorating the first site where the American flag was flown, I pause. Young lovers have climbed the steps encircling the tower; I can hear them alternately quibble and whisper somewhere above me. To my left rises Boston's skyline. Faintly, I can hear traffic noises from Union Square below. Then, suddenly, the lovers quiet, the traffic noises cease, the world is miraculously still.

The stately Victorian houses on the other side of the hill are decorated for Christmas: wreathes, colored lights, mechanized Santas and angels bowing and waving from bay windows. "Take it easy, Jewell-Girl," I whisper to myself as I find myself lingering outside what look like cozy and warm and inviting homes. A sexless college student in a hooded down jacket and thick boots passes me on Columbus Avenue. I am dressed like a recent arrival from the Third World. First stop: St. Gerard's Thrift Shop.

Union Square seems bedraggled to me. In the little park in front of the community access television station, a handsome brick building, once a firehouse, an excited group of teenagers huddle around a video camera mounted on a tripod and shout to one another in Spanish. But other than them and the bustling little Japanese supermarket nearby, the square has an abandoned, unhappy feel to it. There are the usual mysterious offerings placed on the Vietnam Memorial: a wreath that's been in the snow and rain much too long, a tiny plastic dinosaur and a faded peacock feather. The Pigeon Woman stands in front of the liquor store feeding her filthy, feathered friends. She wears a quilted coat, a man's hat – the kind with earflaps – and her go-go boots with striped kneesocks against the cold. Traffic roars past, and the car horns blare the moment the lights change.

But it's warm and cheerful inside St. Gerard's. A little creche scene sits in the shop window beside a pair of gold sandals. The sweet old ladies who run the place chatter to each other as they sort and fold. They nod to me as I walk in. Near the back of the shop, a Haitian woman in a thin cotton dress and a kerchief wrapped around her head paws through the dresses. She grunts at me as I rifle through the coats. St. Gerard's is filled with its usual comforting smells of mothballs, talcum powder, and a hundred different perfumes and colognes permanently sealed into the polyester clothes. Busily inspecting wools and gabardines, a whiff of something, or maybe just the sound of wire coathangers scraping against a clothes rack, something conjures up my mother's sunporch.

My mother.

I try on a fairly new Harris tweed coat, grey, a boring color, but you can't beat Harris tweed for warmth and durability. My mind racing with plans how best to doll up this solemn garment, I inspect the pockets (always inspect the pockets when you buy second-hand; they'll tell you a lot) to feel that unmistakable feel of folding money.

A twenty!

It is obviously an omen. And it also means that the twenty dollars I lifted from petty cash will go a little farther.

Thank you, God.

"Thank you, deah," says the sweet old lady when I pay for my coat. She charged me five dollars. I think she gave me an even bigger discount than usual. I must be looking particularly pathetic today.

I make my way out of the square, up Summer Street to the corner ma and pa store, or "spa" as they're known around these parts, on the corner of Summer and School streets. There's a pay phone in there, the real old fashioned booth type Superman always used.

Pulling the door behind me I settle down and dial Virginia's area code.

She answers on the fourth ring; she's listening to "West Side Story." I can hear Maria and Tony swear their eternal love in the background. One of the very first times she spent with my father, she told me once, he'd brought her to his house to listen to "West Side Story."

"The look on his face as he listened to that stuff," she'd marvel.

But only this minute, sitting in this womblike booth and hearing Bernstein's creation, do I truly understand the look on my mother's face when she'd tell me that story. It's the look all of us have, all of us, that is, who are foolish or wise enough to fall in love with a musician. It's the look when we come to understand that we will never be first in our lover's eyes. That we may have a tiny taste of passion, a sample of ardor, a little something on our plate, but we'll never, ever get to gobble up the whole thing.

"Hello?"

I don't even breathe.

"Hello? Hello? Is anybody there? Is that you, Jewell?"

Click.

The woman behind the counter's yelling at a kid when I come out of the booth.

"I don't cayah if they're for your mothah. I can't sell cigarettes to a minah." It's not a Somerville accent. Down East, probably. I remember her; she reminds me a lot of Florence. So I smile at her, and she instantly enlists my help.

"Am I right?" she demands. I study the kid. He's one of those skinny, skinny, wiry, street punks with the baseball cap on backwards and an ultrawise mouth. Somerville is full of these punks. Listening to this kid, however, as he earnestly entreats her: "My mom. She's sick in bed. Just this once, okay? etc., etc.", I decide he's destined, no doubt, to become mayor of this fair city. An alderman, at least. He's that good. But he's wasting his breath. The spa owner crosses her arms across her chest (she's really bundled up; it's cold in this pokey little store) and just stares him down. To the kid's credit, he doesn't curse her; he just slinks out of the store.

Yeah. Definitely mayoral material.

"It's cold in here," I observe as I pay for some gum. She's got all kinds of stickers and those little magnetic picture holders with kids' pictures in them on the cash register. Christmas decorations cover the wall behind her. Bus schedules are taped next to the door. The counter next to the cash register is covered with wicker baskets full of penny candy. She's listening to some call-in show on the radio; I can hear a male voice whine about seat belts.

"The furnace broke again," she says and, without warning, I burst into tears.

"Well, it's not..."

"I'm sorry," (Ohmygod is this how it's going to be, now? Am I turning into another Nadine?), I snuffle. "I-I-I've been sick, and I seem to just start crying for no good reason. The doctor says I'll get over it soon." As I'm saying this, I notice a wooden stool in front of the counter. And I realize that this woman, with her warm, open face, must be a kind of mother/mother confessor to the people who live nearby. The Neighborhood Shrink.

And I remember how I started crying when I first met Margaret.

Now I'm really bawling. "Can I just sit here a while?"

"Take as much time's you want," she says, opening one of those dinky little tissue packages and handing me one. A different male voice on the radio is talking about gun control. If it weren't so chilly in here I could stay forever. But just as I settle myself, a Spanish-looking young man, his dark hair carefully combed, carrying his maroon supermarket jacket bustles in: "Gimme a Herald, will ya?" he says not unkindly but impatient, lordly. Self-important. As if bagging groceries were the most crucial thing in the world and he's running late. I get down off the stool.

"Thank you," I say as I open the door.

" Keep warm," she says. Wahmm, she says. It's the sound of a woodstove and oatmeal with butter and maple syrup, of thick socks, sturdy boots: of backwoods Maine. Standing in this chilly corner spa, I know for a moment that I am truly in New England.

Once outside as the arctic wind knifes through my new coat, I almost turn around again, I almost go back inside. I stand at the corner of School Street and Summer (ha!), I watch the lights change from red to green and to red again, until I am sure of what I want.

I want, as a woman I knew a long time ago once said, I want a "whiff of testosterone." Decidedly. I am ready, now, for the smell of cigarettes, the pungent odor of men in wintertime, the heady aroma of sweat and wet wool, of mud with a tad of manure mixed in, and spilled beer. I'm hungry for low, deep voices and a football game on the television set. Most of all, I crave that drop-dead moment when I first walk in: the longing eyes, the way they suck in their guts when they realize I'm attractive and alone and ohmygod, that's real red hair, the approving looks they exchange with one another, that tension, and the to-die-for power, that control, as I slowly begin to walk towards an available seat. Most of all, I'm starved for that delicious feeling in my belly as I fill myself with their hunger, their palpable need. How my body asserts itself beneath my clothes. How my breasts, my nipples, the muscles of my inner thighs feel as I move across the darkened, and now, hushed room. Yes! That's what I want.

With my head down and forward as a bulwark against the cold, I begin my trek back to the square. Head bent low, I can't avoid seeing the trash, the garbage along the sidewalks and encrusted into blackened snowbanks: bits of plastic, bits of styrofoam, bits of rusted metal, shattered glass. The street lights have come on now, the Christmas lights, as well. Salsa music from deep inside a triple-decker reaches me as I walk past. My leg begins to ache; I have to slow down. A group of boys play in the vacant lot where an ancient brick school used to be; their curses fill the air. I cross Summer Street. My leg is really hurting now. It takes me longer to cross the street than I'd thought. An oncoming car with only one headlight guns out of the square and has to slow down a little.

"Retard!" the driver, a young woman with a lot of hair screams at me through closed windows as I scramble over a snowbank and onto the curb.

And a drink. I'll let him, whoever he is, buy me a drink. Just one. Jack Daniel's. That's what I'll have. Just one. Just so I...

A furtive movement raises my head. I'm passing the Multi-Service Center, a large brick church building like the one next to Esperanza Place, and home to several human service agencies. A sparrowlike creature huddles on the front steps.

"Jewell?"

I walk closer. It's Shannon.

"He hurt me real bad this time," she says. I can see her face, now. She's pretty banged up; I can smell whiskey on her breath.

"Let me take you back to Esperanza Place."

"They'll never take me back," she mumbles. Looks like she's lost a tooth.

"Sure they will," I say bravely, although I have an immediate vision of Dell slamming the door in both our faces. "What are they going to do? Throw us out into the cold? C'mon, we'll grab a cab in the square."

We stumble along the sidewalk. In front of the Chinese take-out place on Somerville Avenue we find a waiting cab. Shannon reads the driver's ID as I stuff her into the blissfully warm back seat.

"Bertrand St. Louis," she says. "That's not a name, that's a city! Fuckin' Haitians. Why don't they-"

"Just shut up, Shannon. Okay?" I say. And, thankfully, she quiets.

53

The driver pretends he didn't hear her. But he did, he understood. I can tell by the proud, skillful way he negotiates the maze of East Somerville streets, the care he takes at each turn, each red light. We're back at Esperanza Place in ten minutes. Margaret opens the front door, takes one look at Shannon and declares: "She should be in detox." Florence starts calling around for an available bed. There's none to be had.

"Quick! Get the bottle in my desk," instructs Florence. I know just where it is; I saw it this morning. So I run to get it. Shannon's eyes are beginning to look truly scary. The two women practically pour the stuff down Shannon's throat.

"Let's try psych emergency," suggests Florence. They bundle Shannon up in about a million blankets and take her to the car.

"You're in charge," Margaret shouts to me as they drive away. MX is beside me. He looks up at me with newfound respect as I shut and lock the front door.

"You hear that, MX?" He softly pads behind me as I check windows and the back door. "You better watch yourself because I'm in charge." He follows me from room to room. "Do you think anyone noticed it was missing?" I ask him as I slip the twenty back into Florence's drawer.

And the pounding begins. "Shannon! I know you're in there!" It's The Neanderthal.

MX races to the front door and begins to growl, then bark furiously. The pounding stops.

Thank you, God.

The pounding has brought the others downstairs.

"He could still be out there. You better call the cops. Tell them to escort Florence and Margaret home," suggests Nadine.

"Good idea," I say. We locate the three of them at Cambridge City, call the cops, then huddle before the TV until Florence and Margaret come home.

"Shannon's going to be all right," reports Florence. "She had a seizure, but she managed to not hurt herself."

"You gonna take her back?" asks Nadine.

"Good question," says Margaret. "I suggest we discuss it at meeting tomorrow."

"What a night," says Margaret as she wearily climbs the stairs.

"Thank you for your help, Jewell." She starts to go into her room." And, yes, I did notice the money was gone."

"I returned it."

"Well, let's consider it a loan, shall we? Can you guess what the interest's going to be?" She's grinning at me.

Looks like I'm going back to school.

Chapter 8

I move myself slowly up, up, up through dank and brackish water – foul smelling, sickly green – toward the surface, toward the light. The drowning dream, again. I awaken choking, sweat-drenched, and already tired.

They're at it again downstairs. "Someone used my cream cheese," Dell screams; the refrigerator door slams. "What's it take to keep my fucking food?" she demands. I hear her clearly as I reluctantly leave my warm bed and make my way to the bathroom. "Huh? It was clearly marked. What's it take? I'm sick of this shit." She stomps up the stairs.

"Have a nice day," Shannon calls after her sarcastically, then says something in a lowered voice. Dyke, probably. That's what it sounds like. She and Nadine snicker.

Yes. I know. It's hard to believe but it's true. Shannon's back. After endless Should-We-or-Shouldn't-We-Take-Shannon-Back discussions, we finally decided NO! That she was too much of a risk to all of us.

"What's the matter with you people? Are you brain dead? Her boyfriend's come here twice! Don't you get it? He could come here some night and blow us all away!" Dell argued. Dell has a way of getting right to the heart of the matter. But, after all of that, the decision was taken out of our hands, anyway.

It happened like this: First, there wasn't a single available bed to be found in any of the battered women's shelters. (This was all going on while she was still in the hospital.) Well, all right, we decided, how about finding a home through Friends Meeting at Cambridge? A "safe house." But while that plan was being implemented, Shannon's boyfriend, The Neanderthal, the "fathah of her children" was locked up again, this time for a good long time. So we could at least relax on that score.

There was still, however, the issue of Shannon herself. Did we want to live with her?

"Well, on one hand. . ." Nadine began bravely but when she'd mentioned five or six different hands, Tasha broke off from trying to burp Jordon to say, "Look, we can't be arguing this thing to death. Shannon's gettin' outa detox tomorrow. We gotta decide one way or other." She vigorously patted Jordan's tiny back for emphasis.

And as it happens sometimes, we became quiet together. Even Jordan, who nestled on his mother's shoulder. So quiet I could hear icicles dripping outside, purple finches at the bird feeder.

And I could see Shannon curled up on those cold, cold steps, the way her head rolled back and forth when we were in the cab. So I said what I truly believed: "I sure as hell would hope you'all would take me in if I needed you."

And so, as usual, Dell pulled it all together: "Okay," she said briskly, "let's do this. We let her back in, but she's on probation. She messes up on curfew, leaves the kitchen a mess – stuff like that – she's outa here. Okay?" We nodded in agreement. Margaret left the room visibly relieved.

So Shannon has returned to our nest. But her attitude since she's been back more than makes up for the absence of a madman pounding at our door. She's truly a Pirate Princess these days. A member of royalty. A royal pain in the ass.

"They're always like this when you let them back," I heard Florence say to Margaret the other evening. They've taken to holing up in Florence's office after dinner. Sometimes they laugh so hard together the whole house can hear them. Those two can really hoot it up, especially when we've had a rough day. And since Shannon's been back, seems like they've all been rough days.

"They're always like this," Florence repeats. "I hope you know what you're doing."

"Why is that?" Margaret asks lightly, ignoring Florence's last remark. She's not ready yet to admit it was a mistake taking Shannon in.

It hasn't been curfew or chores Shannon has neglected: she throws herself into her tasks with an almost frightening intensity. Rather, it has been her attitude that has set all our teeth on edge.

56

Yes. Attitude. Shannon knows she's received special treatment; this awareness has proven toxic to Esperanza Place.

Someone – probably Nadine – has told her it was I who stood up for her (though, when you really think about it, I was just advocating for myself!). So now, most nights, when everyone else has gone to bed, Shannon comes to my room and in her high, nasal, hollow voice, tells me her story again and again. Now perched on the edge of my bed, now pacing back and forth, now examining my haircombs and makeup, her face scrubbed clean, her hair pulled into a topknot, she speaks as if what she's saying didn't really happen to her but maybe to someone she knew a long, long time ago. She stares at herself in my mirror, she tells me over and over about her father, about the mean streets of Charlestown, about her kids.

"...and Justin, he's really smart, ya know. Did I show you the Valentine he made me?" I nod helplessly. She has shown it to me every night this week. No matter. She again pulls the now-limp bit of red construction paper out of her pocket. Silver glitter sprinkles to the floor. "Will you look at that? See how he writes his name. And he's only five. He's really smart," she says woodenly. "And Tiffany, now..."

"So is his mother," I break in. She is. Spooky smart. Shannon inhales every self-help book she can get her hands on; I never saw anyone read so fast or so hungrily. When she went for her GED, she scored a perfect score on the Literature and Fine Arts predictor test. "Margaret cried when I told her. She cried!" Shannon reports, clearly puzzled by Margaret's reaction.

I can understand Margaret's tears. Sometimes, listening to the distractedness, the emptiness behind Shannon's words, I find myself reacting for us both. If she can't feel or show that she's truly experiencing what she's talking about, I reason, I'll do it for her. It's very confusing.

Equally confusing is how all her zombielike tone falls away when she's talking about anyone but herself. If she's analyzing Nadine or Dell, for example, she's a different person: steely, insightful, compassionate, and able to quote whole passages from the psychology books she's read. But I am without experience in these matters. I know nothing of intimate chats in my room, of confidences, of friendship with another woman. The last time a female sat on my bed was when a classmate from school came over to my house. I was about twelve. My mother threw a hissy fit for some reason, and my friend went home early.

And I'm too embarrassed by my lack of experience to even discuss my confusion with Florence or Margaret. So I nod and I smile, all the while feeling like some kind of human sponge soaking up all of Shannon's pain. But, somehow, mysteriously, she squeezes me dry again. There seems to be no rest for her, no peace, no satisfaction that she's said these things again and again. The same sad story begins the very next night.

But the most confusing part is that every night when, at last, Shannon goes back to her room, I ask myself the same question: Why am I still here? Why am I putting up with this shit ? My leg has mostly healed, so why haven't I moved on? What's keeping me here? I have no idea.

"Hey! Jewell! Ain't today the day you go to SCALE?" Shannon asks as I stumble into the kitchen.

"All them big words you use and you never finished high school?" demands Nadine. "I never knew that!"

"Ooops. I guess I let the cat out of the bag. Sorry, Jewell," Shannon says in her usual none-of-this-affects-me way, and she kind of turns away and goes back to reading the paper.

"You knew I didn't want anyone to know!" I explode. "What kind of friend are you?" I walk around the table so that I can look directly down at her. "Forget it, Shannon. You hear me? Just forget it!" I scream in her face. "Don't come near me. You got that? I mean it." And just for a moment she looks up at me and just for a moment I see pain in her eyes. Now it's my turn to stomp upstairs.

Dream-bruised, nauseous, and generally pissed, I stumble onto the Broadway bus. When I'm angry like this, tapes play over and over in my head, and I can't seem to be able to push the Stop button. This time the tape is about something Shannon said to me last night. "Of course your mother knew about you and Mr. Allen," she said confidently. "Mothers always know."

I get off the bus across the street from the Powder House Community School, an imposing stone and concrete elementary school, and walk through the schoolyard to Holland Street. It's recess time for the younger children. Their teachers, four of them, stand at the edge of a large, fenced-in area the size of two basket-ball courts, a large mound of filthy snow piled at one end. Each woman stands identically to her colleagues: her right foot slightly forward, her weight on her left leg, her arms tightly crossed on her stomach. They look bored, chilled. "Get off that snowbank," they take turns yelling.

A group of children, two boys and three girls, dressed in brightly colored snowsuits, play some game whose rules are mys-terious to these thirty-year-old eyes. From what I can see, the object of the game is to run, run like the wind from one end of the play-ground to the other and scream as you do so. It doesn't seem to be a race, no one seems to be IT, the children don't grab or touch each other. All that seems to be happening is an obvious joy in running, a delight in shrieking.

I round the corner and there it is. SCALE is in what was appar-ently once an old-fashioned brick public school, three stories tall, now renovated, which houses several different organizations and programs.

I stand outside with a group of shivering smokers and watch the traffic flow. As I stand there, a series of buses pull up to the entrance: little, half-sized orange school buses with "Head Start" painted on them disgorge screaming, little kids; a regular-sized bus full of old ladies (where are the old men?) slowly climb down the bus steps and make their way inside; women in padded-shoulder business suits alight from a Tufts University van just as flocks of brilliantly plumed Haitians and Brazilians and Central Americans, all chattering to one another, exit.

I walk inside and down the stairs to what must have been the school's basement and is now SCALE. I wait for the dreaded smell of school to assault me, the smell of erasers, crayons, pencil shav-ings, sweat. But all I can smell is cheap perfume. At the bottom of the stairs is a large, open area with corridors going off to the left, the right, and to the back of the building. A large blue and white banner over the tiny waiting area explains SCALE's initials: Somerville Center for Adult Learning Experiences. Beneath this banner sits a hooded black man; I could hear the tinny sounds from his Walkman as I came down the steps.

"I have a 2 o'clock appointment with Irene?" I explain to a

harassed-looking woman sitting at a desk in the tiny, crowded office to the left of the waiting area. She gives me the briefest of smiles, then her phone rings. "Good afternoon. SCALE. May I help you?" The phone rings again. A pregnant woman in a navy blue maternity jumper, red turtleneck, and Birkenstocks with thick, black and white striped socks kind of wanders in: "Has anyone seen…?" Two other women at the office's other desk are hunched over a computer screen and arguing with each other. Another phone rings.

"Walk down that corridor. First door on your left past the GED department," instructs the receptionist. Her phone rings again.

I follow her directions, walking past a group of maybe fifteen, twenty people as they line up outside a large room. It's like a scene from one of those World War II movies, you know the one I mean, the mail-call scene with all the different names: "Yablonsky. Adams. Rabinowitz. Torres." Only this scene incorporates men and women, young and old; there's even a guy in a wheelchair. These people, apparently about to take a GED test, look particularly grim.

When I am at last sitting in Irene's tiny, windowless office and we've finished chatting about my "delightful" accent and Margaret and what a wonderful woman she is and I've filled out a bunch of forms and discussed my educational history ("Completed 9th grade" Irene writes on one sheet), I decide to put an end to this farce.

"I can't do math," I announce to her.

"Many of our students have difficulty with math," Irene says. She is a beautifully dressed and coiffed woman of about my mother's age.

Your mother knew. All mothers know.

"No. I'm not talking difficulty. I'm talking impossibility. I'm talking…"

"That your mind goes completely blank and you feel dizzy and completely stupid and helpless?"

"That just about sums it up."

"This is an adult learning center. We specialize in - can you believe it? - adult learners. Many, many students come through these doors with math anxiety."

"But…"

"Well," she says, getting up from her desk. "Let's see how you do on these predictor tests, first. They'll give us a pretty good idea how you'd do on the real thing." She leads me to an empty classroom and shows me how to fill out the answer sheet. Since there are five tests, I am only to take two, today. Literature and the dreaded Math.

The windowless room smells like after-shave. Ezra wore that kind, I remember. There are a couple of posters on the bulletin board. One exhorts me to READ! The other poster tells me not to get AIDS.

Okay. It's a deal.

The Literature test is not that bad. A lot of "It can be inferred…" and "Which of the following would the author be least likely to support…" kinds of questions. Tricky but not impossible. The Math test is all word problems, those horrible little situations that you have to solve. Since there doesn't seem to be a choice for "Who cares?" on the answer sheet, I guess as best I can.

And the results are in. I only missed four questions in Literature. And the Math?

"Tell you what I'm going to do." Irene says. "Instead of putting you in a regular GED class, I'm going to assign one of our math teachers to work one-on-one with you."

That bad, huh.

My Literature score is so strong that Irene sets up a time for me to take the real GED test next week. "And I'm sure you'll do just as well on the Social Studies and Science and Writing tests," Irene predicts. "Give my love to Margaret," she adds.

I am so excited, so punch-drunk happy, that I make a series of wrong turns and instead of walking the short distance to catch the bus on Broadway, find myself on a street named Corinthian. Corinthian Street? Yes!

"When I was a child, I spoke like a child, I thought like a child, I reasoned like a child; when I became a man, I gave up childish things. For now we see in a mirror dimly, but then face to face. Now I know in part, then I shall understand fully, even as I have been fully understood. So faith, hope, love abide, these three; but the greatest of these is love."

My grandmother made me memorize that passage. And right there, in the middle of Corinthian Street, I burst into tears from the sheer wonder and craziness of it all.

Chapter 9

Lily Farnsworth has asked to come to our meeting for worship this morning. She has not made any direct contact with Esperanza Place since she stormed out of here six months ago. Except to mail us a check every month. In her absence, her silence, our benefactor has assumed mythic proportions for all of us. But the woman I greet at the door just before 10 o'clock is not at all the angry, condemning Amazon I remember, but, rather, a frail, wispy old woman.

"We're glad to see you," I say to her pointedly. I can feel her body heat clinging to her heavy winter coat as I hang it up and almost waiver in my resolve to let her know what she's put all of us, especially Margaret, through. She studies my face to see if my accusatory tone was intentional. So I look directly at her. "It's been a long time," I add, just in case there is any doubt, and gesture towards the library.

The others have already gathered: Margaret sits alone on the love seat and is already deep in prayer as we enter. She looks up briefly, gives Lily a grateful smile, then shuts her eyes again. Nadine curls up at her usual spot at one end of the couch; Shannon occupies the other end. They both watch Lily warily as she carefully sits in the upholstered chair. Tasha sits on the oak rocking chair and nurses Jordan; she seems to nurse him all the time. Florence hunches over in the straight-backed chair and kind of grunts to herself at our entrance.

We're all nervous. No one says a word the entire hour, not even Tasha, although every once in a while Jordan makes little sucking sounds and then, later, cries briefly before falling asleep. Instead, we listen to the sound of our collective breathing which, even though I fight it every time, controls my own. I don't seem to have a choice in the matter. Every meeting for worship, I come in here determined to not get pulled into the whole thing and within ten minutes, I'd say, I'm breathing in exactly the same rhythm as everyone else.

And, like every morning these days, I pray for someone to say something, anything. Please! Nadine? Dell? Help me. Fill this room with your silly words. Let me become distracted by your trivialities, your half-baked truths, the petty details of your pathetic lives. For ever since Shannon's pronouncement, the silence has become unbearable for me. "Your mother knew. She knew."

What Did My Mother Know?

Like an essay question for the GED, I see these words on the top of a blank sheet of paper. I'm to fill in the lines. But unlike a GED topic, which somehow elicits from me an orderly arrangement of statements and supporting details all nicely tucked into paragraph form, I can produce nothing but fleeting images: Mr. Allen's pudgy hands, my freshly laundered underpants neatly arranged in my top bureau drawer, and a time – yes! This keeps coming up – when, miserable and ashamed, I lay in my bed after one of Mr. Allen's visits and I sensed my mother standing in the hallway just on the other side of my closed door although she made no noise. I felt her there, smelled her there. I felt her. . .what? Helplessness? Fear? What?

What Did My Mother Know?

I imagine a scene; it's the bedtime story I've been telling myself almost every night lately. In it, my mother, huge and powerful and absolutely terrifying in her white-heated rage, looms over a sniveling, quaking Mr. Allen and flails him with her mighty tongue. Oh, she is awesome, my mother, as she confronts my perpetrator. The names she calls him! The abject guilt she produces! Lovely.

In the light of day, I see so many things I could long for, so many other ways the scene could be played: castration, torture, public humiliation, some kind of financial restitution. But this little fantasy, sad as it is, possesses such power, it can lull me to sleep.

And then, mercifully, we are squeezing hands to indicate meeting's over. "May I have a word with all of you?" asks Lily as we're starting to stand up. We sit back down.

"I have a great deal to say. So please make yourselves comfortable." We grab pillows or any available places on the couch and chairs. When we're settled, she continues: "Perhaps you'll remember how upset I was the last time I visited here. I want you to know that I've done little else these past few months but reflect on that moment when all I could think of was getting out of here as fast as I could."

She looks into each of our eyes, then smiles ever so slightly. "I'm an old woman. I've seen many things. Poverty, discrimination. But until that day when I sat here with all of you, I do not believe I ever contemplated evil before. For that was what it was. I felt chilled and frightened and very badly shaken. Somehow, evil has... brushed past me. When I was working at the Blue Hills Settlement House and saw what people of color experience on a daily basis, I always seemed to be able to excuse it all. 'Oh, he or she just doesn't know any better,' I'd tell myself when I heard stories – terrible stories! – of injustice and cruelty, unspeakable bigotry. But until that morning here with all of you, I firmly believed that with education, adequate health care, and, of course, money – the usual things we've always done to help people – any social ill could eventually be overcome. Certainly it was that sort of thinking that led to creating this shelter in the first place.

"I've been doing a great deal of reading since I last saw you. Perhaps all of you know – I certainly didn't – that Freud had a similiar reaction to mine when he realized how prevalent incest was. I'm not excusing either of us. But to learn that incest, sexual abuse is so widespread... it was a shock."

"Imagine our surprise," says Dell sarcastically.

Lily ignores her. "Hitler, Stalin, Pol Pot – apparently they were too far away, too removed, too abstract for me to feel. But I want you to know that I have been feeling nothing else since I left here so abruptly." She adjusts her sweater a little.

"And now I see, or I guess I should say, I imagine sexual abuse everywhere! It's gotten to the point that I can't bear to see a father touch his child, or any adult interacting with any child. It's terrible! And terribly unfair. But I suppose what has happened is that since I have spent a lifetime in blissful ignorance, I am now compelled to be extraordinarily vigilant."

She retreats inside herself for a moment, so I study Lily Farnsworth's face. It's a good face: prominent cheekbones, alert blue eyes, a strong chin though jowled, and remarkably few wrinkles. Her skin is tanned in sharp contrast to the rest of us.

64

And then, seemingly, she remembers where she is. "Has this happened to you?" And she looks at us with a kind of wide-eyed vulnerability, a kind of childlike faith that is almost not to be believed. But there it is, right smack on her weathered face. I am beginning to like Lily Farnsworth.

We nod.

"How are you about men?" Dell asks as if Lily were some kind of laboratory experiment.

"What do you mean?"

This is happening way too fast.

"Do you find yourself walking down the street and hating each and every one you see ?"

Lily gulps a little, then answers: "I'm very suspicious of them, I suppose. Very wary. Even men I'm very fond of - men at Meeting, that sort of thing."

Ah, yes. We nod, again. For once you admit that the world is not what you'd been to taught to believe, once you admit that innocence is dead, once you acknowledge that evil exists and just might be sitting right next to you while you're riding the T, pushing a shopping cart, then, my friend, you are ready to admit that someone you know might be a perpetrator. It's a logical progression.

And if we are truly being logical here (although at this dizzying pace I am not at all confident we are), then there follows the next logical question. Indeed, I feel the question hover in the room as, thankfully, a silence at last descends upon the group.

And you, Lily Farnsworth, what is your story? Could it be that the real reason you became so upset is that something was stirred up in you? A vague memory, perhaps? A mysterious, recurring dream suddenly made shockingly clear?

But no one, not even Shannon although we lock eyes briefly and I know she's thinking the same thing, no one dares to voice the question, and so it is absorbed by the silence.

She continues to explain: "It's like I've stumbled into some strange, terrible place. And I'm not sure how long it is I am supposed to stay here."

There is quiet and then Florence speaks: "There's a story – more like a fable – floating around these days." She pauses to catch her breath and, consciously or not, we all settle in our places. "Once upon a time, there was a small village beside a river. One day one of the villagers looked out and saw a baby coming down the river on a raft. So the villager quickly jumped into a boat, rowed out on the river, and rescued the baby. He brought it home to his wife who agreed to care for it. The next day, another villager saw another baby and the same thing happened. The next day there were three babies on three rafts who were saved and the next day there were five. Every new day brought more and more babies until finally, the entire village was doing nothing but saving babies. They were so busy, no one had time to go up-river and find out where all those babies were coming from." She looks at each of us. "I think we're discovering where all those babies are coming from."

Lily stares at Florence for a moment. And suddenly I understand that this visit and whatever comes next (she's already reaching into her overflowing canvas bag for a manila folder) have been carefully orchestrated and that Lily Farnsworth wasn't prepared for any in-the-moment kinds of responses, no matter how insightful. That the way she plans to cope with this vision of evil is to do just what she said she always does: throw money at the problem.

"Yes, well…" she bustles, opening the folder. It's full of newspaper clippings, magazine articles, some original, some Xeroxed. "I've been doing a great deal of research on the subject of Healing," she begins, pronouncing the word as if it, all by itself, possessed magical powers. "There's a man from Vermont, a released Friend named John Calvi who is doing some awfully interesting work. I think we should…"

But she's interrupted by Margaret.

"Wait a moment, Lily," says Margaret. "This is going much too fast. I, for one, am going to need a little time to digest all that has happened here this morning." She pleads with our benefactor with her eyes.

"Then I'll just leave these things with you, shall I?" asks Lily, and she carefully hands the manila folder to Margaret.

Sometimes there are moments when you can see another person whole. When I look at Lily Farnsworth, I can see an elderly woman who, because she's wealthy, sees the world from a position of comfort and orderliness in spite of her experiences in Roxbury. She can't help herself. There's a kind of contentment about her, almost a smugness, but also a well of goodness, a great pool of light-filled love and caring and all that good stuff (probably made possible by her easeful, peace-filled life), which just shines out at you and lets me forgive her quirks and abruptness and general bumpiness. She means well; she truly does. And of course, it's always easier to forgive someone who is rich.

And I think about the woman I saw on Somerville Avenue yesterday morning, a mother – maybe Greek, maybe Portuguese – wheeling a beat-up baby carriage full of flapping clothes on her way to the laundromat, two small daughters anchored at her skirt. Haggard, obviously poor, perhaps raising those children alone, her life seemed especially harsh to me because her children's faces were living, breathing testimonials to the beauty she once clearly possessed. Those children's lively, bright eyes, their dark, sleek hair, healthy skin, the sturdy way they carried themselves, so like and yet so unlike their mother, all seemed to mock the exhausted woman walking between them. How bitter she looked, how worn out, how used up.

Like my mother.

I see my mother in her navy-blue robe with the breast pockets that look like arrows. She's standing next to my grandmother's car, her face drawn, angry.

"I just need a little time to myself. Is that so terrible?" she says defiantly.

"God will-"

"Mother! Don't do this to me!"

I snuggle beside my grandmother. The car smells of White Shoulders and righteous indignation.

"Can I offer you some coffee or tea?" asks Margaret, interrupting this reverie. But Lily turns this down, and then our benefactor leaves. All of us remain in the library.

"So!" exclaims Dell. ""What's in the folder?"

"Articles on incest and sexual abuse," says Shannon in her usual flat tone while skimming through the pile with impressive speed." Fathers. Step-fathers. Mothers. Priests. And healing." She pauses to glance at a few clippings. "Some of this stuff sounds pretty out there. But this one sounds good." And she holds up a magazine article.

"Hold on," says Florence. "Before we start any kind of new approaches, we gotta all get to the same place. As I understand it, the first thing that has to happen in the healing process is wanting to heal. You gotta sign up, so to speak. You or I or Margaret or some psychologist doesn't just tell someone, 'Okay, now we want you to do this and this and that.' It'll never work."

"Why don't we…" begins Tasha but she is interrupted.

"Some of us like how we're dealing with all this shit," Nadine blurts out. "I love to eat. No matter how much my therapist and I talk about food and emptiness and psychological hunger and craving sweets, when I'm having a flashback, all that stuff's out the window. All that therapy stuff? That's dead. A Snickers bar makes me feel better. Two Snickers bars make me feel a whole lot better! I love Snickers. And I don't ever, ever want to give them up." Nadine stares hard at us.

"I think each of us needs time to reflect," Margaret offers after a period of quiet. "It's like what Florence said. We need to get to the same place. And I think we need to get to that place together. It seems to me that this has to be a collective effort. In the future, of course, when new women come here, it would be different. But for those guests here, now, Esperanza Place is simply a shelter. A roof over your head. Meals. Sure, everyone gets to meet with a therapist if you want. Some people have to go to AA meetings. Jewell's going to start school, soon (Groan). And meeting for worship. But I think we all need to, like Florence said, sign up. And it sounds like we're not ready to do that. Not this morning, anyway.

"While all of this is fresh in our minds," continues Margaret, "I suggest we spend some time by ourselves thinking about all of this."

"Yeah," Nadine chimes in. "Like those old Quakers making people in jail spend time thinking about their crimes."

"You think this is a penitentiary?" asks Florence. She's a little huffy; there's an edge to her voice.

"I am more than a little penitent," Shannon says so softly that only I hear her.

Margaret faces Nadine. "You're right, of course. Early Quakers believed that if, instead of being beaten and starved, people in jail were to be punished by sitting alone and pondering their crimes, that this was progress. People in jail would contemplate their sins by sitting in what they began to call penitentiaries. Those early Quakers believed that what they were doing was a more enlightened approach to our penal system." She laughs in that self-deprecating way of hers. "It didn't work, of course. For the same reason that Lily's plans about this morning didn't work. You must be the ones who decide to change. To heal. And she hadn't thought of that."

She picks up the folder. "Something will come out of all of this. But we don't know what it is yet."

And as if orchestrated, everyone except Tasha gets up and leaves the room. She remains in the rocking chair, the sleeping Jordan on her shoulder. Her face is dreamy as if her rocking is for herself.

I go upstairs and sit on my bed for a few minutes. Nothing. Those poor convicts. I wonder if anyone gave them anything to read while they were supposed to be reflecting upon their crimes. And could they read, anyway? I try the lotus position on the floor like Tasha does but it hurts too much. I go over to the window, stare at the billowing plume pouring out of the power plant smokestack, but that feels like cheating. So I stare at myself in the mirror.

My mother liked to tell the story – in fact it was the story told of me when I was a little girl, the story told at family gatherings and at the dinner table: The Jewell Story – about how once, when I was maybe four or five and crying about something, how I dragged a heavy chair across the floor in my bedroom so I could watch myself cry. Heavy chair, mind you. For some reason, that chair's bulk was a significant part of the tale.

The mirror gives me back my face. It tells me my hair no longer falls out in clumps. It shows skin and teeth. And that is all that I can see.

I think about what Nadine said about Snickers bars and all the different ways I and Nadine and Dell and Tasha and, yeah, even Shannon, have survived. And I think about thistles.

I remember a time when I was out in the country with a bunch of white guys who'd grown up in the 'burbs, were addicted to pot, played Bob Marley covers, and called themselves a reggae band. I was living with the drummer then, a sweet, kinda dopey guy named

Marty, paranoid as hell, always thinking I was making fun of him because I used bigger words than he did. I usually didn't do the road trip thing, but it was a Fourth of July weekend and Marty and I were living on Mission Hill and I was sick of the city. So when I found out that they were playing some gig in Amherst and that someone in the band knew someone who was living in a farmhouse near there and that everyone was planning to stay out there a couple of days, I tagged along.

It was a beautiful summer day, I remember, and everything smelled good. After breakfast (cooked by someone else's girlfriend, of course), I smoked a joint, then went outside for a walk by myself. Marty was still in bed. The screen door shut behind me, I remember, making that perfect, creaky, summer noise that conjures up lemonade and the thwack of tennis balls and sultry, sweaty lovemaking on top of the sheets. The farmhouse, one of those dilapidated affairs you find in the country, the kind covered with those ugly, brindle-colored asbestos shingles that in no way resemble bricks, was surrounded by corn fields. "Knee -high by the Fourth of July," someone had said at breakfast. And so it was.

The cicadas were already buzzing although it was still pretty early, and there wasn't a car or a truck or a boom box within earshot. I was walking down this country road, wearing a lacy, old-fashioned, calf-length, cotton slip I'd bought in a vintage clothing shop, powder-blue espadrilles, a beat-up straw hat and feeling fine!

About a half a mile down the road, I came upon a thistle bush almost as tall as I am. A real monster of a plant sitting beside the road with formidable prickly leaves – I very gently touched one – and flowers of the sweetest shade of purple and those thousands and thousands of little wispy parachute kind of things that must carry thousands and thousands of thistle seeds all over creation.

"Consider the thistle!" I said out loud. I was very stoned and, like all very stoned people, believed I had discovered the Meaning Of Life. Or, in this case, the Meaning Of Survival. I mean, here was this plant, which not only covered itself with leaves with tiny, nasty barbs all over them so no one would want to get near the thing to eat it or cut it down, but it also made thousands of seeds that got spread around every time the wind blew, and it also had these sweet little pretty flowers that attracted bees, I imagine, which somehow also helped to keep the thing alive and thriving.

Just like rats and cockroaches, there will always be thistles.

Dell has used her bristliness to keep going, Nadine cushions herself with fat, Shannon drifts along whichever way the breeze is blowing, Tasha makes another creature to keep it all moving along, and I – am I the seductive flower? Or am I really another Shannon.

Healing. I'm supposed to be thinking about healing, right? And what I am thinking is this: Maybe I have already signed up. After all, what other possible reason is there for me to still be here?

Chapter 10

The minute I see him my heart sinks. He's just what I expected: tall, gangly, with a straggly beard, longish curly brown hair, and a bad haircut. His eyes are an as yet unspecified pale color – I don't want to inspect them too closely – and he's wearing a frayed sweater and rumpled corduroys. A worried expression, which just might be permanent, creases his forehead and saddens his eyes. He takes a good hard look at me, then smiles. It's a nice smile (he has good teeth), genuinely warm and accepting. I notice he carefully avoids shaking my hand.

"We're going to work down here," he says; his voice is low and very gentle, almost hesitant. We walk down the learning center corridor to a tiny room with a round table and two chairs. There's a tape player on top of a file cabinet in the corner.

"How 'bout a relaxation tape while we work?" he asks. He's grinning at me.

"I'll try anything." So he mashes the Play button, and what sounds like wind chimes and some sort of flute music, kind of nondescript and kind of boring, fills the room.

"Let's start with a kind of diagnosis –" He breaks off, looks at me ruefully. "I'm sorry. I just broke one of my own rules."

I just stare at him. He smells like Chinese food.

"It bothers me when teachers pretend they're doctors and use words like 'diagnosis' and 'prescription.' I'm a teacher; what I do is figure out what you need to learn and how you learn best. Anyway, try these, okay?" He hands me a sheet of paper.

"Which weighs more: a pound of feathers or a pound of lead?"

is the first question. Well, that's easy, enough.

"Estimate how many people are in this room."

"Is this a trick question?" I ask. And he blushes. "I usually use this with a class. Okay," he says, taking the paper from me, "try this one, instead." And he writes something, then hands the paper back to me.

"Estimate how many cups of coffee you drink a year." Now, that's not too hard, either.

Next, he hands me a deck of cards, a calculator, and a piece of paper and a pencil. "Okay," he says. "There are 52 cards in this deck. If you were to pass them out to three people, how would you figure out how many cards each person would get?"

"I'd divide 52 by 3," says I.

"Okay, show me how you would do it." So I put 52 inside the little box thing, then divide. "There would be one card left over," I announce. He's writing stuff down.

"Suppose you did it on a calculator."

"I don't know how to use one," I say and he writes this down.

"What if you were to actually deal the cards. How would you keep track of how many each person would get?"

I think for a minute. "Well," I say slowly. I'm not used to this kind of mushy, slow, anything-I-say-is-right math. "I guess I could keep track like musicians count off measures – one two three, two two three, three two three, right up to seventeen. Course you'd have to say seventeen real fast so it would fit into one beat."

Now the guy is grinning at me like I'm a genius. And hands me a piece of paper. A test. It's pretty easy: common-sense kinds of questions, estimation, and a few division problems with two numbers on the outside of the little box thing which I skip because I can't remember how to do them. We go over the answers together-every once in a while he'll ask me how I came up with a particular answer but when I look at him blankly (I don't have a clue how I did it), he just smiles and, finally, stops asking.

"Pretty pathetic, huh?" I say.

"No," he says, very kind of drawn out and carefully, "I wouldn't say that. I think you have great potential."

"Yeah, right!" I sneer.

But he ignores me and starts right in teaching me how to do

long division. After about five minutes, when I am still getting all mixed up, he says: "Okay, Jewell. Let's try something else. I want you to write down the symbols for the steps." So after he refreshes my memory (for the nineteenth time), I put down the symbol for divide, multiply, subtract. . .

"What do I use to bring down the next number?"

"Make up one. This will be very helpful when we do algebra."

"I am never doing algebra." I state.

"Sure you are. So. What's the symbol?"

I think for a few moments. "There." I say, and draw a pathetic-looking pail.

"Sort of like 'Jack and Jill'?"

"You got it."

So now as I'm struggling with a problem, I'm looking at the little symbols, too, and by the end of the hour, I can do two -digit long division!

Now I realize that this accomplishment will not get me a gold medal but, let me tell you, up to this point, the only thing I thought I could get right happened in bed. (The idea of hopping into bed with Zachary - that's his name - makes me want to puke.)

We walk back to SCALE's entrance, stopping by the copy machine so he can run off some homework for me.

"This wasn't so bad," I tell him as I get ready to leave.

"You're a good student," he tells me. "You should get it pretty fast, now." And, again, he carefully does not shake hands.

"See you next week," I say, then head for the ladies' room.

"So whataya have tomorra ?" inquires a voice in the stall to my left. It's a young voice already hardened by cigarettes.

"Writin'. I hate that stuff; where to put the fuckin' periods 'n shit? You?" answers a similiar voice at the end.

"Readin'."

"So how you think you did?"

"All right, I guess. Some of this shit I never seen before. I guessed on most of 'em. Excerpt. Excerpt? What the hell's that?"

"Yeah, I know," soothes her friend. Their toilets flush, the doors open. I wait until they leave before I venture out. I don't need to see what they look like; I already know; they look like me. The big difference, of course, and one you can't see, is that I'm living in a shelter and they're not, probably.

Not twenty minutes from this place is Harvard Square. They've got a building there – I've seen it – with the word "PHILOSOPHY" written over the arched doorway in big letters. Not twenty minutes from here, people are reading thick books, they're arguing over some picayune point as if their lives depended on it, they're writing science equations on a blackboard, clattering away on their computers. Do any of those folks over there know we're here? Do they comprehend that there are people like me who don't know the difference between a comma and a decimal point? Do they have any idea how much we don't know?

A window has been opened for me in this windowless, basement school. Just for an instant. It's like I've been cooped up inside all my life and then, boom, all of a sudden, I catch a glimpse of the ocean or mountains, the World Trade Center towers. And in that instant I can see with terrifying clarity how much I have been shut off from. How much I don't know. How much more there is that I've never even heard of.

"So how did tutoring go?" asks Margaret when I return.

"I'm not going back," I reply.

Chapter 11

Shannon's disappeared again. Out the door. I should have seen this coming. I should have said something.

For the past week she's been more than hyper. She's been sitting on my bed talking a blue streak, saying any dumbass thing that came to her head.

"Ya know who you should go out with, Jewell?" she'd say, her words spilling out in one long breathless heap. "One of those guys who works for a funeral home. Ya know the kind I mean? They're really gorgeous, and they wear those perfect suits and their hair is all slicked back but not greasy, ya know, just perfect. And they have this look on their faces. Like they're really trying to be sad and all, but all they're really able to come up with is 'Heh! How do I look? Aren't I unbelievably gorgeous?' I can just see the two of you together somewhere, both so gorgeous, so perfect, so…"

"Just shut up, will you?" I'd interrupt night after night. "I was asking you, again, for the forty-thousandth time, for you to explain to me why you believe my mother knew about Mr. Allen."

And night after night she'd simply change the subject: "Ya know, you really should get yourself HIV-tested," she'd say. "With your history, you're a high risk. There's a place in East Cambridge. No name."

"I don't want to even talk about it," I'd tell her but would she listen? Hell, no. Shannon told me everything she knew about AIDS two nights running. Both times without seeming to catch her breath throughout her entire monologue.

I should have told someone. I should have done something.

That same week, she started going to AA meetings daily, sometimes two a day. She up and joined a support group at the battered women's center in Union Square. She asked Florence about starting therapy. She was the one who prayed the loudest at our meetings for worship.

"Dear Spirit," she'd say, all earnest and intense, "it's really gonna work this time. I'm gonna get my kids back someday soon, I just know it. It's all coming together for me. I can feel it. Help me, dear God."

And there were a couple of times when the light was just right, or maybe because the moon and the stars were just where they were supposed to be and I didn't have a sheet-soaking nightmare the night before and Dell was in what passes for a good mood, a couple of times I did actually believe that she would pull it all together for herself. Margaret beamed at Shannon; it all seemed to work.

But most of the time when I looked into her eyes, I would remember who I was looking at: thistledown. Or some kind of fast-talking, fast-moving shell. There's this big hole inside Shannon, a yawning, aching hole as big as the Grand Canyon that gets filled up only in small, precious moments. Little, tiny spaces of time when she is whole.

Hole. Whole. Shit.

I should have said something. I should have tried.

So. After about a week of this manic behavior, she simply vanishes. Poof. No one in the house even heard or saw anything. And all her stuff was still in her room.

Right away there was something spooky about this disappearance.

We all started talking about her in the past tense only a couple of days after she'd gone. We hadn't even noticed it because each of us did the same thing. Florence pointed it out to us during a meeting for worship. And then, when she'd been gone a week, the phone calls started coming in: women from her support group, women who'd stayed here before, friends. "Have you heard from Shannon?" they'd say.

Spooky.

Sure enough, about a week after that, Nadine spotted a little piece in the Somerville Journal about a woman's body having been found in the vacant lot on Summer Street. "I wonder if it's Shannon," she asked in an I-hope-I'm-wrong voice as she shoved the paper across the breakfast table to Margaret. It was a beautiful day, I remember, one of those early spring days when the wind is warm, not chilling, and you begin to believe that winter might actually end someday. A cardinal was singing away in the back yard; sunshine poured into the kitchen. Nothing bad can happen on a day like this, I thought. Yeah, I actually believed that.

So right after breakfast, Margaret drove to the police station near Union Square. "They were very nice," Margaret reported later. "Very gentle." Her body slumped in her chair as she told us; her hand shook as she stirred her coffee. The cops showed her photographs of the dead woman's clothing. It was Shannon.

She'd been severely beaten, of course. Somehow the police figured out she'd been battered to death in one place, then her body had been moved to the rubble-filled lot. Some kids had found her. Or so the cops said.

No, it hadn't been The Neanderthal. He was still in Billerica. No. It had been someone else. Women like Shannon and me, we have a real gift: We can walk into a room of strangers and find the one man who's going to beat us up. Kill us. It's a knack we have.

Shannon had been on her own since she was fifteen, so there was some difficulty finding the appropriate people to notify. Margaret finally managed to locate Shannon's mother in a housing project in Charlestown.

"As thin and intense as Shannon," Margaret reported. "Only with dyed red hair and fewer teeth. Smoked like a chimney. Kept saying something about Shannon's brother, too. It was awful."

All of us were getting pretty worried about Margaret. After the initial frenzy of activity with the police and Shannon's family (there was the gruesome task of contacting Tiffany and Justin but, thank God, Margaret was spared this last responsibility; someone from DSS had to), she holed up in her office for hours.

And still the phone calls kept coming. It was getting downright spooky. "Have you heard from Shannon?" a wispy female voice would ask. Or maybe it would be a social worker from a detox center. Shannon had been in and out of a lot of them. And Margaret would have to go through the whole thing again.

"I have to say something even though it's gonna make me look like an asshole," said Nadine one morning after a couple of weeks of this. She had clearly picked her moment; Florence was home sick and Margaret was in her office interviewing a prospective new guest. Nadine, Tasha, Dell, and I sat around the kitchen table addressing envelopes for Shannon's memorial service. Jordan was asleep upstairs. We stopped and listened. "I'm sick of 'Shannon this and Shannon that,' " she said, somehow managing to look both defiant and sorrowful. "Shannon had this way of getting everyone's attention – maybe it was all that pacing around she did – so that if she was in the room with you, most of the time everything was directed towards her. And now, even though she's dead, it seems like she's still the center of attention around here. And I'm sick of it. What about me?" She started crying.

No one said anything. MX snuffled around under the table, then put his head on each of our laps while looking up at us with those big ol' brown eyes. One by one we pushed him away until he finally gave up, ambled to a corner, and lay down with a loud, dramatic sigh. And still no one said a word. True Confession Time? Even females who are supposedly more evolved than men when it comes to expressing our feelings don't know what to do, sometimes, when someone says something so raw. We couldn't even look at Nadine.

"I'm really glad you said that," began Tasha after what felt like hours. "I been wanting to say something like that myself. I know we ain't supposed to say anything bad about the dead and all, and I feel really bad the way she was just lying there in all that trash and all, but you're right. I'm sick of it, too."

Chapter 12

The mountainous snowbank on the Mass. Ave side of the Porter Square shopping center shrinks, more purple finches call in the back yard, and cardboard eggs and bunnies decorate doors and windows in the neighborhood. You don't see many heating oil trucks now. DeMoulas' sells bunches of droopy, green-tinged daffodils for $1.50. Spring is just around the corner; you can smell it in the damp, chilled ground.

Florence parks the van on Brattle Street right in front of Longfellow's house. It's a huge, yellow mansion, a kind of a monument to success and being adored and honored in one's lifetime and, yes, complacency – qualities I never, ever associate with the life of a poet. Poets live in garrets, don't they? Poets suffer. There is not a hint of suffering in this columned home with its lawns and now-dormant lilac bushes all around it.

Our group crosses Brattle Street. Facing Longfellow's house is a long, narrow plot of grass, a kind of a village green. This is Longfellow Park. It was created so that the author of "Paul Revere's Ride" could have an unobstructed view of the Charles River. Or so Florence explains. This green is circled by yet more huge, elegant eighteenth-and nineteenth-century homes. And a Quaker meetinghouse.

It's a slate-grey day in late March, still pretty chilly, although a little warmer than it's been. I can hear a robin somewhere but I can't see it. The tops of crocuses can barely be seen coming up in the tiny flower bed near the entrance to the brick meetinghouse. We go inside, hang up our heavy coats in a little vestibule. Then, as a kind of clump, we walk into the meeting house.

Friends Meeting at Cambridge is both sparse and muted: The walls are an inoffensive blending of sand and putty, the cork tile floors a predictable shade of dark brown, the lighting minimal. Everything – the long benches, the bench cushions, the tall, unadorned windows, the light fixtures, the colors of the walls, the flooring, even the fireplace where a hearty fire flickers and crackles – everything seems to have been carefully chosen to be of excellent quality, while at the same time not to draw attention to itself, its cost, its placement, its very existence. "Pardon my dust," as my grandmother used to say. Please, please, don't give your surroundings a second thought.

The benches, long enough for maybe six or eight people to sit, are placed in rows against the four sides of the meetinghouse with an aisle leading from the vestibule doors to the center of the space. Which means that everyone faces the center of the room. And each other. Dell decides for all of us where to sit; Nadine's feet shuffle along as we cross the entire length of the meetinghouse to sit together on a first-row bench near the fireplace.

There are maybe twenty-five or thirty people here. Shannon's mourners seem to fall into three distinct groups: Quakers, social worker types, and Shannon's friends. The Quakers are older men and women, mostly women, dressed much like Lily Farnsworth, who sits among them. She nods to us, smiles. These Quakers sit quietly with their heads bowed as if to say: this is how it's done at a Quaker meeting.

Shannon's friends, men and women, numbering maybe ten or twelve, are in their early twenties. Most of them wear jeans and sweatshirts. One woman, as thin as Shannon, is dressed completely in black including heavy, heavy use of black mascara and eyeliner around her startling blue eyes. They're an unhealthy-looking lot: missing teeth, pasty complexions, too fat or too thin. They sit on a couple of benches across from us, nudging each other and whispering loudly.

The social worker types wear silk dresses or suits with shoulder pads, stockings and heels. They're not in their element, either; you can tell. But at least they're being quiet about it.

I am relieved to see that Tiffany and Justin are not here. There had been a rumor that they might come. I don't think any of us could handle that right now.

Margaret slumps on a bench across the room from us like an old woman. Defeated. Her lovely eyes filled with pain, she fusses with a burnt orange shawl tightly wrapped around her stooped shoulders as if she can't get warm. A lovely, long arm reaches around Margaret's shoulder, straightens her shawl. Who is that?

A woman about the same age as Margaret sits beside her. She is dressed in an embroidered batik dress, her hair cut short with wispy tendrils framing her narrow, handsome, tanned face. Her hair is that peculiar color when a natural blonde becomes middle-aged: something between blonde and white, a kind of faded yellow that looks almost like silver in some lights and gold in others. One of those tall Sigourney Weaver types. I hate her.

And I don't have to even give a second thought as to why. It's her proprietary manner with Margaret. They're lovers. You can just tell.

Just as I stare at her, she stands up. "My name is Hartley James. I have been asked to explain a little about what will happen here this afternoon for those of you who might be new to a Quaker meeting," she begins in a clear, patrician voice. Very self-assured. Very Brahmin.

The restless, giggling mourners stop moving. They straighten their backs, look up at her with expressions remarkably close to fear. There is something of the schoolmarm in this tall woman's voice. Something challenging, unforgiving. And for a moment I am almost sad for Margaret; this love affair is not a solace for her. How could it be?

"This is a meeting for worship in thanksgiving for the life of Shannon Daniels. Those who wish to may speak out of the silence about Shannon, what she meant to you, what you are feeling in your heart. A handshake will close this meeting." Then Hartley James sits down, smiles at Margaret.

Gratefully, Margaret smiles back at her lover, although pain wraps around her as tightly as her shawl. It is Margaret's palpable sense of loss and regret that focuses my thoughts. I am forced to remember why I am sitting in this lofty-feeling room in the first place.

Shannon. Skinny, jumpy Shannon. Spooky smart. Bullshit artist. Able, in a kind of a in-a-mirror-dimly sort of a way to sense what was denied her, but never really able to pull it all together for herself. Broken. Running on empty. Alone in a crowd. Murdered and abandoned. Dead.

I concentrate on Hartley's words. (Hartley? What kind of name is that?) And a miracle happens:

To speak out of the silence. This phrase I've heard a hundred times suddenly means something. Somehow, with the comforting sound of a fireplace fire and sitting with a group of people seemingly focused on the same thought, somehow, this idea of opening my mouth, giving voice to my thoughts in the context of silence feels very different. My thoughts are like a four line poem lovingly set in the middle of a largish page of creamy, thick vellum. The words, elegantly framed by the luxurious space around them, are significant only because of the not-word page.

Or:

The silence is an ocean of incredible depth and wonder, horror and madness, too, and we're swimming in it; it's all around us and through us, but it's the same ocean for all of us, it feels the same, is the same temperature for all of us sitting together in this wet-wool scented room. And when we speak it is because we've been fed and bathed and buffeted and chilled by this ocean of silence. Our words come from the same place.

Swimming in it. For months I've been swimming in something else: an issue, as Nadine's therapist would say, an awareness of something wrong, something pervasive and ever-present. A dull, achy, chronic pain. All of us at Esperanza Place have been eating, drinking, sleeping, talking of what seems like nothing but the topic of abuse. Of incest. Of dirty, sordid little secrets. We've all been swimming in it.

But this afternoon I'm swimming in something else. It's a miracle.

And a deepening silence gathers the room, and we are all breathing in rhythm to one another, and in some mysterious way we are reaching out to each other. Yes, even the callow youths of Charlestown are reaching out to me and I to them and Margaret and, okay, yes, Hartley. And, yes, the social workers. And to Tiffany and Justin, too, even though they're not here. The crackling fire, as if responding to what is being experienced, ceases to crackle. The logs settle with one final burst of noise, like a sigh, then quietly glow.

We sit like this for maybe ten minutes, and then the young woman in black suddenly jumps up. "I don't even know why I'm doing this?" she begins, ending her statement as if it were a question. "But it's like I'm supposed to, you know?" And she looks at Hartley for corroboration. Hartley gives her a you're- doing- just-fine look, and the young woman continues. "I knew Shannon from a day-treatment program at Mt. Auburn. There were maybe eight or ten of us in our group, but Shannon was always in the center of it, you know? She had a way of grabbing everyone's attention? Just coming into the room? And I used to resent that, the way everyone did that to her, the way she was always the one who got all the attention? But you know, sitting here just now, I've been thinking how she was a kind of a weird gift?" Again she looks to Hartley. "Like you said before? About thanksgiving for her life? Shannon had a really shitty life. But she was so alive, she had so much energy! She taught me about just being alive?" She savors the word as if pronouncing it for the very first time. "It's really sad she couldn't teach that to herself." And the woman in black sits down.

That this stranger says the same thing we'd said among ourselves (but with a little added-on something, of course) has an amazing effect on Nadine, Tasha, Dell, and me. We look at each other kind of guiltily as if we'd just been found out, somehow.

And then the second miracle occurs:

I absolutely know that all of us are thinking the same thing. That we're going to tell Margaret we're ready for Lily's manila folders now. That we're signing up for God knows what. That we're going to try.

Just then, as if planned, one of the social worker types stands, clears her throat, and begins to read from a sheaf of papers she holds in her trembling hands.

"Shannon Daniels was a very special person," she begins. But I don't listen. For I am caught up in the wonder of these miracles and, at the same time, really, really bothered – no, angered – by this grey-haired, well-dressed woman with her crimson-framed glasses who, by reading from something she probably labored long and hard at, is saying something about trust. No, no, that's not it. But by not letting herself speak spontaneously, by not letting herself just stand up and say what is in her heart, especially after what that other woman just said, she is saying something to me about how she can't trust herself to do that.

So I don't care what she says. Even if it's well written.

I think about how once, in English class, when I was in ninth grade, this very, very heavy girl wrote about what it's like to be a fat teenager. I can still picture her standing in front of the room reading her paper out loud, her chin quivering like she was crying but she wasn't. Her essay wasn't what is considered well written in Lynchburg. In other words, it wasn't filled with words like "enhance" or "abiding" or any other multi-syllabic word that rolls off the tongue. No. She chose simple, plain words to tell an honest, painful truth.

She got a C+.

The social worker sits down, and we settle into a deep and abiding silence. The fire glows. Someone coughs. Several coins fall out of someone's pocket. Someone giggles.

And the third miracle happens:

I become aware that one of Shannon's friends is staring at me. Yes! He's sitting directly across the room from me. Nice looking. Now he's smiling at me. From here, it looks like he's tall, certainly he's skinny. He's got dark eyes, an olive complexion, longish, feathered hair like a heavy-metal head. Looks like he's missing a couple of teeth. But nice looking, anyway. His shoulders droop a little, though.

In about the same time it takes to try on a coat, I try on him. I see him swagger up to me. I know how he walks. After this meeting, while we're all standing around outside, he'll come up to me. I know it. I see me doing the magic I do so well. I see Margaret standing a little off to the side with Hartley; I see her almost flinch when he reaches over to touch me. Maybe he'll brush my hair from my face or lightly tap my shoulder. Whatever the gesture, it'll be gentle yet dangerous. Intrusive. Too quick, too soon. But I, so hungry for touch, I move closer to him, tilt my head in a way so that he'll want to touch me again.

And again. And again. And again. And in the silence I see waiting for phone calls and tentative conversations and, as clearly as I see the people in this room, I see those dark eyes that burn for me presently (Yes, it's true. Nadine sees it. She nudges to me, whispers: "Check out that guy across the room! He's in love with you. Look!") become dull. The fire ebbs, dies. I see boredom. I see the hand that gently stroked my hair become a fist.

No. I'm not buying.

I close my eyes, lower my head. And although it feels as if I were just delivered from evil somehow, and what I ought to do is mumble the Lord's Prayer, what I do instead is to gratefully whisper the

Twenty-third Psalm. But in a new way. A way I've never been able to experience before. Certainly not in Sunday School class. Something (Someone?) compels me to change all the pronouns:

The Lord is my shepherdess, I shall not want.
She maketh me to lie down in green pastures
She leadeth me beside still waters
She restoreth my soul.
And I feel something inside me begin to move and grow.

Chapter 13

I'm so sick of healing I could spit. Every day, now, it seems like we're trying something new. Strange, weird-tasting food appears on our plates. Worse still, mealtime now means endless conversations concerning diet and nutrition and vitamins or the latest study someone's read in the Globe or one of the health magazines we now receive by the carload. Workmen materialize to put in raised beds in the backyard so that we can begin gardening. Dance therapy, massage, art lessons, sessions with Nadine's shrink: a bewildering menu of choices and possibilities is now being offered to us. Trouble is, none of us has a clue what to do.

My sense is that if Margaret were in better shape, all this new stuff would be handled in a different way. But Margaret is just going through the motions these days. She took a few days off after Shannon's memorial, and she and Hartley went to some island I never heard of in the Caribbean. When she returned, tanned and well rested, she seemed like her old in-your-face-cares-about-you self for a while. But then the weather turned again, the chilled grey days returned, and Margaret has retreated into herself.

She talked about it only once. It was at a meeting for worship, and Margaret sat, drawn and alone, wrapped in that shawl of hers. "We will get through this, you know," she assured us in a voice deepened by her pain and also by the effort needed to break through that pain to speak to us. "We will endure."

But her pronoun was all wrong. We were not suffering. Only she was. Margaret was doing such a thorough job of mourning Shannon that somehow we all just let her do it for all of us. Which was fucked up, of course, but damn, she made it so easy!

So Florence runs the show and seems comfortable with a kind of scattergun approach to the ideas and experiments in Lily Farnsworth's manila folders. "Just try it," she urges, her broad, honest features softened by her pleading. And she shoves some article or book into our empty hands.

Which is why I find myself gingerly lowering my body into the frigid water of the Tufts indoor pool. How come an indoor pool's so cold? How am I supposed to heal under these conditions? Huh?

To make matters worse, I am sharing a lane with a pathologically cheerful young woman. "Sure," she practically shouted, her voice echoing off the tiled walls, when I asked her if we could swim together. As I stood shivering in the shallow end, she climbed out of the pool, grabbed one of those paddleboard things, adjusted her goggles, pulled her black Speedo down over her perfect butt, gave me a patronizing smile, then dove back in over the glowering me.

I hate her. I hate Florence. And Margaret. I hate my mother. And Mr. Allen and Dell. (I'm swimming now. Slowly. Very slowly.)

And, no, I didn't do one stretching exercise before getting into this icebox. Not like these long-thighed men and women in their skinny, skinny suits who decorate the sides of this goddamned pool. I believe they're just showing off, is all. Preening. Making their muscles ripple. Not me. I just start pawing at the water. Doing the only thing I know: the sidestroke.

And I hate the new woman – Rose – and Margaret's bitch lover...

Change the tape.

These black and white tiles I inch past were probably laid, one by one, by hand. Men from Somerville, I would guess. Wonder what their reaction would be to Little Miss Cheerful up there (Jesus! She can swim. She's practically at the other end of the pool, already!) Were they simply grateful for the work, those men? Grateful someone had decided to line this great big ol' pool with tiny tiles that ought to be in a bathroom, maybe. Or did they curse a world where inane blondes from Connecticut or California or somewhere glide past their handiwork without a thought.

Well, I'm thinking of you, guys. I'm taking the time to study each and every one, okay? (Pick the apple, put it in the basket, throw it away and glide. Pick the apple, put it in the basket, throw it away and glide. Pick…)

My partner is now coming past me. She gives me a wide berth and a quick smile. Give it a rest, girl. You don't have to have everyone in the world love you. Total adoration is not required. And since your daddy's paying $20,000 a year for you to be here, you can bet I'm never going to like you. So stop trying.

(Pick the apple…)

I learned to swim at the Y in Lynchburg, the only kid in the class whose mother wasn't sitting along the side of the pool knitting and chatting and waving to her offspring. One of those knitters, Cecelia Sydnor, was a neighbor. Her daughter Amanda was a couple of years behind me at Bedford Hills Elementary School. Mrs. Sydnor had offered to drive me to and from class. But I refused. I took the bus by myself. All these years later, gliding slowly in the Tufts pool, I'm wondering what possessed me to turn down something like that. Why did I do that? It would have been so much easier, especially when it got cold, to have Mrs. Sydnor chauffeur me.

What did my mother know?

Change the tape.

I'm beginning to feel longer. My body feels stretched, sleek. The water moves around me, holds me. I'm in the water, through water, water ripples past my eyes, my body feels the rhythm of my arms and legs, my neck trusts my arms and legs to pull me through the water; my neck relaxes. My eyes lower almost to the water's surface. Like some gnarly alligator with her fierce eyes searching the fetid swamp for prey, so do I move through these chlorinated waters, my eyes open, alert, powerful.

My ears are submerged. Faintly, I can hear reggae sounds from the lifeguard's radio, splashes from the other swimmers, and, more clearly, my own steady breathing. My innards align themselves. I feel my insides shift as if being borne by water allows my stomach, liver, intestines to move ever so slightly back to where they want to be.

I fart. The gas bubbles under my suit. No one notices, no one cares. I am alone inside this perfect body. I am fully alive. I am happy. My stroke isn't beautiful, but I'm steady. Fifteen minutes later when I triumphantly pull myself out of the water and make my way down the stairs to the sauna, my legs wobble a little, but I feel wonderful.

The sauna is paneled with some kind of sweet-smelling wood. Against two sides double-tiered, very wide benches have been built, wide enough to let arms and legs rest where they may in this hot, hot, bone-warming room. There are two other people in the sauna, an older man in peppermint-striped bathing trunks reading a very wrinkled copy of "The Washington Post" and a very thin, young woman wearing two bathing suits for some mysterious reason. No one talks.

Just as I spread out my towel on the top tier, Rose bursts in, bringing her own irritating self and a blast of cold air as she struggles with the sauna door. She fusses with her towel, gives one of her woe-is-me sighs, and I remember why I am supposed to be doing all this swimming and relaxing in the first place.

Don't get me wrong: At first I truly did feel sorry for the woman. Older than the rest of us and far more worn out, she came to Esperanza Place with a purple and black eye and one tiny suitcase and moved into the spare room next to mine. Maybe in her fifties, maybe only thirty; you can't tell with women like Rose. She's hard to pin down. DSS took her kids from her, three of them, because she couldn't protect them from her boozy, violent husband. Sometimes she says that. Sometimes she has four children. Sometimes she says she was the drunk. Sometimes she says she grew up in Southie, sometimes rural Maine.

But it's not her slippery ways that get me. Hell, we all leave a story better than we found it. Anyone believing everything I say's a damned fool. No, it's those slumped shoulders, the hangdog expression, her washed-out blue eyes and stubby eyelashes, her lifeless, thinning hair in its old-lady tight, tight curl style, her pink scalp clearly seen between each curl, the way she plops into a seat as if she weighed two hundred pounds (she's bone thin, really), how she scuffs her feet like a nursing home resident on her last legs. That's what gets me.

And now, lying here in this sauna as she still fusses with her towel and I feel my body go limp in this all-soothing heat, I am forced to admit to myself that it's more than "what gets me." To be honest (and it's ironic that it's forked-tongue Rose who makes me want to be totally open about this), there's something about the woman that makes me want to smash her face. Her eyes, her voice, her frumpy body say to me "Beat me. Hurt me. It's all I deserve."

There. I said It. Without getting too explicit about how I'd do it, what it would feel like. I just know that what I feel is so.

"Phew! It's really hot in here!"

Thank you, Rose, for that insightful comment.

"I'm gonna take a shower," she says and starts to get up.

"Please try to not let the cold air in again," says Miss Two Suit in a real snotty voice. For a moment I almost feel sorry for Rose, but she just assumes her tortured expression and slinks out. And yes, she does struggle with the door again and yes, she does let another annoying chill into the room. Ms. Snot snorts impatiently, takes a few sips from her water bottle (like she's in a marathon or something!), then rolls over onto her back.

I contemplate how, when you're well-off and life is pretty much okay, a blast of cold air while you're lounging in a sauna is a totally different experience from what I know. We're all recovering from something, I guess. We're all marking the moments since: since that last drink, since we broke up with that bastard, since we were ill, someone died, got that paper cut. And although I know my pain has much greater meaning in the great scheme of things, that if I and Ms. Snot over there were to appear on Oprah, I'd have the audience making those female cooing sounds of sympathy in no time flat and that they'd sneer, they'd just hoot at whatever's eating her ("Oww, you only got a B- on your last paper? Why you poor, poor thing, you!"). Just for this moment, as I lie here warm to my bones, I am able to believe that no one's pain should ever, ever be trivialized.

I roll this over in my mind as I roll myself over.

Later, in the shower, I try not to stare at the other women's bodies. Ms. Snot is here, her naked body revealing deep tan lines. She pretends to ignore me, but she's checking me out, too. I can tell. My body smells of chlorine but feels tight and strong and powerful. Rose is already dressed.

She and I walk out of the women's locker room and head for the exit. But when we walk past the workout room, we stop to watch a blonde pony-tailed woman in black spandex, wearing a Walkman, do the treadmill. How long has she been on that thing? There is certainly not an ounce of fat on her long frame. What can she be thinking? There is something about the mindlessness of what I'm seeing (she certainly doesn't notice us; just stares straight ahead and walks, walks, walks) that I find totally infuriating. My newfound equanimity flies right out the window. Even Rose is moved to whisper as she nudges me to move along: "Is she for real?"

We trudge up College Avenue, walk over the railroad bridge, which seems in dangerous disrepair, then successfully make our way across an insane intersection where four streets converge, yet there is no traffic light – just ineffectual stop signs, which everyone ignores. It is early evening and the sky is a dark, dark blue. As we walk down the hill toward the Powder House rotary, we can see a crescent moon above the Tufts playing fields. A slight breeze brings the smell of warmed earth toward us. It feels wonderful to be in an open space, to feel expansive in this cheek-by-jowl city.

"Let's walk on the field for a little bit," I say.

"It'll be all muddy," whines Rose.

"What's a little mud?" I ask. "C'mon." Reluctantly, she follows me through a gap in the chainlink fence, and we walk on grass. Mushy grass, admittedly, but nevertheless, the real thing.

Suddenly, from behind the bushes we hear a low moan followed by the unmistakable sound of a man urinating. Rose giggles.

And then, there he is, coming toward us at a menacing speed. He's young, strongly built, with the thick neck and broad shoulders of someone who works out. Wearing a sweatshirt, sweatpants, and a baseball cap worn backwards, he gives us a drunken grin.

"Hi there," he begins. Rose and I, without as much as looking at each other, start walking real fast. But the muddy ground slows us down.

"Aww, c'mon, don't be like that," he enjoins, effortlessly trotting along beside us. "There's a great party going on back there..." he carelessly points in some unspecified direction. "Whyncha come?"

Somehow we both know enough not to say anything. There's another gap in the fence ahead, we speed up, head toward it, but suddenly he pushes his way in front of us so he's blocking our escape.

"I said don't be like that!" he says, angry now. There's a twang to his voice; the southwest, maybe?

"Leave us alone," I say. My voice, constricted by fear, sounds laughably weak.

"Leave us alone," he shrilly mimics. Now he's close enough for me to smell his beery breath.

I try to push my way past him: "Fuck you," I say; the only weapon in my pathetic, female arsenal. Pathetic. So, of course, he slaps me across the face, and I fall backward; Rose helps break my fall into the mud. She starts screaming.

"Hey, I'm sorry," I hear him say as he takes off.

"What happened to you?" Dell asks when we get back.

"I don't want to talk about it," I snarl.

But of course we do talk about it. We process. The women at Esperanza Place process. I am repeatedly asked if I want to meet with a therapist so we can process. I refuse. I meet with Margaret. She and I process. Endlessly. What could I have done differently? What could I have said instead of "fuck you"? How could I have not placed myself in this situation? Had I put myself at risk? Was this a pattern? And blah blah blah. Finally, after a couple of weeks of this, I finally burst out with: "C'mon! The guy was a jerk. Just some dumb, drunk kid. It was no big deal." So everyone drops the subject.

Of course, I still secretly cry about the whole thing in my room every night, I still play a mental video (three cameras, good sound) a thousand times a day, I still fantasize about what I would have done if I had been carrying a gun. But most of all, I secretly seethe at the alacrity, the ease with which everyone accepts my bald-faced lie. Because it was a big deal.

Hey, I wish I could tell everyone. It was something and I'm really hurting, but I'm also really embarrassed that you all are still talking about what happened to me. So I'll just say this appeasement thing, okay? But I don't mean a word of it. Please! Don't listen to my words. Take care of me still. Especially now, now that I've given you permission to forget about it.

* * *

Yolanda wishes to make five sets of curtains. If each set requires 3 1/3 yards of fabric, how many yards does she need altogether?

"All right, now," Zachary says for the umpteenth time. "Will your answer be larger or smaller than 3 1/3?"

"Larger. Five times larger. This is a multiplication problem."

That's right. I'm back in school. I reenlisted. Part of the healing thing. I have successfully passed four of the five GED tests. Only the Math remains.

"But," I quickly add (he has that satisfied look on his face again; it will never do for him to think I'm getting any better at any of this), "I can't remember how to multiply fractions. Do I invert or something?"

"What's one-third of a yard?"

Lessee. One third. Hey! I get it!

"One foot."

"Good! Now how much is five times one foot? Picture a yardstick in your mind. You want five 'one foots'."

"So, it's one yard and two left over. One and two-thirds."

"You're getting better and better at this, Jewell. And you didn't even have to invert."

"Well, maybe, but I still get distracted by the whole thing. Like Yolanda. What kind of fabric does someone named Yolanda choose? Dotted swiss? Lacey ones, maybe? And besides, you keep asking me questions so I can think my way through these stupid things. I'm not at all sure I'll be able to think this way when I'm on my own."

" 'Course you can. I'm just talking you through these, as you call them, stupid things. When the time comes, this kind of thinking will be second nature to you. Honest." He pauses a moment, then adds: "I saw you the other day. At Foss Park."

"Well, I didn't see you."

"I know," Zachary says firmly, as if acknowledging that he'd been purposefully staying out of sight. For I was clearly the wide-eyed tourist that day, drinking in the scene, bedraggled as it was, as if I were witnessing some great event. I get like that, sometimes. Like I'm some kind of human recording device. That I somehow can and must hear, smell, see, taste everything as intensely and unflinchingly as possible.

"C'mon," Margaret had said, looking up from the paper at breakfast. "Let's go see Paul Revere this morning. It'll be fun."

Of course, we all whined and complained. Although it was, just like Longfellow's poem says, "the eighteenth of April," the weather seemed more like February. "It's cold. It's nasty out," we reminded her but to no avail. "Dress warmly," she said. And that was that. I think we were relieved that Margaret wanted to do something. Even if it sounded stupid.

A chilling wind blew grit into our eyes and trash along the gutter. I watched a neon-orange potato chip bag bounce down the sidewalk in front of us. Sometimes I imagine a series of scenes around the city, quick shots of, say, the old people getting out of their vans at the senior center on Holland Street, just two or three seconds' worth, then a scene in DeMoulas' parking lot where all kinds of families – Haitian, Central American, Somalian, Brazilian, Greek – in all kinds of beat-up cars and vans vie for the same parking space, then to the statue park in Davis Square, and so on and so on. And in each scene, the same piece of trash like that empty potato chip bag would blow across as if connecting the whole thing.

"Why did you decide to start a shelter in Somerville?" I asked Margaret, kicking the bag into the gutter. "Why not out in the country somewhere? This city is so ugly!"

"Well, the truth is, we went around and around on that one. But we finally decided we wanted to be near other services, other agencies. And we wanted to to be in the midst of things, not isolated somewhere. Someone from Cambridge Meeting had bought the house years ago while going to Harvard Divinity School. It was large enough, near a bus line, and to be really honest, I think there was something about the grittiness of the neighborhood which appealed to the trustees. Esperanza Place is real, if you know I mean. "She flashed a smile. "You'll see, Jewell. You'll miss this part of town, someday."

"What do you mean?"

"You'll be moving on soon, don't you think?"

We stopped for the light at Broadway and Cross Street. Margaret looked over at me, waited for me to answer. I shrugged my shoulders as the light changed and we began to cross. She shook her head and joined the others.

A crowd of about fifty people had gathered at Foss Park to await Paul Revere's arrival. Surrounded on three sides by busy highways and woefully lacking in trees or shrubbery, Foss Park is not so much a park in the classic sense of sylvan, quiet, and designed by Olmstead, but rather a not-city kind of a place. Foss Park feels like an open space grudgingly left alone after developers filled every available inch of the city with two- and three-family houses built cheek by jowl beside existing homes and businesses. The park has a public swimming pool, a small playground, some playing fields, and in the shadow of the elevated interstate, some tennis courts.

A red, white, and blue bunting-decorated reviewing stand stood at the edge of the park. In front of this stand was a small parking area; in front of this parking lot ran Broadway, a two-lanes-on-either-side-of-a-median-strip kind of city street. The listless crowd stood in this parking area; an elderly woman in a floor-length calico dress with a navy-blue wool, hooded cape over that and one of those white, lacy caps like Martha Washington wore was speaking into the stand microphone. She appeared to be giving a history lesson, which no one seemed to be listening to. For one thing, it was difficult to hear her above the traffic din. For another, everyone seemed to be more interested in staring down Broadway towards Charlestown. Behind her sat several men who, by their affable expressions and careful scrutiny of the crowd, appeared to be politicians of some kind. They listened to her. At the foot of the stand stood several bored, shivering members of the Somerville High School band, their instruments limply held by their sides. The plate glass windows of the Dunkin' Donuts across Broadway from us were all steamed up.

"Can't we wait over there?" begged Nadine to Margaret.

"He'll be here any moment," promised Margaret.

Sure enough, maybe four blocks down we could see the flashing blue lights of police cars and behind them, a fast-moving dark brown form. As they got nearer, I could make out a horse and rider. They were really booking.

The police cars crossed the McGrath Highway, then carefully pulled into the parking lot. Mothers and fathers grabbed straggling children and made way for the police and the galloping horse.

"The British are coming! The British are coming!" the young rider in a three-cornered hat shouted to us. He was really into this;

you could tell. So was his horse. They pulled up hard in front of the reviewing stand. I love the smell of horse sweat, the creaking sound of a saddle. One of the politicians handed Paul a rolled up scroll kind of paper. "…to the good people of Medford…" was all I could hear him say to Paul.

"The British are coming, the British are coming," the young man said urgently. Like don't hold me up, fella. I'm on an important mission. He grabbed the scroll, impatiently waited for his motorized escort to get sufficiently ahead of him, then galloped up Winter Hill, still shouting his warning to the stores and traffic along Broadway. We watched as he stopped briefly at the tiny little park at the top of the hill on the corner of Broadway and Main Street. Then he turned down Main and was gone.

And just for a moment, I could see where I stood as it must have been in 1775. The Mystic River, now obscured by I-93, was in plain view in this vision, the asphalt and cement lifted, carted away to reveal fields, marshland, trees, farms. Perhaps it was at that moment that Zachary saw me? When I was all caught up in one of my, as my grandmother used to say, reveries? Oh, dear.

But if it were, it doesn't appear to be a problem. For the man sitting beside me looks at me with unmistakable longing.

"Zachary?" I say as gently as I can.

"When you're finished testing, maybe we could…"

"Do you honestly think that'll happen in our lifetime?" I ask.

"I sure hope so," he answers.

I just stare at him. I'm at a loss. So he puts his hand on top of mine. My instinct is to pull away; clearly afraid he's overstepped some boundary line, he begins to lift his hand. There is the briefest motion to separate. But this simple act of flesh upon flesh, warmth upon warmth, this whisper of intimacy, so tantalizing yet so safe, electrifies both of us. Our hands remain where they are; we allow ourselves to look into each other's eyes. And I am suddenly and piercingly aware of how lonely I am, how long it's been since I was gently touched by a man.

I pull my hand away, grab my books. "I'll see you next week, okay?" and make a dash for the door. But Zachary leaps up.

"No. Wait! I've upset you. That's not what I wanted to do. I…"

"I know what you want to do. Let's just forget it, okay? Pretend it never happened."

"Do you want to continue working together?"

"What's the big deal? You touched my hand for about five seconds. It's not like you tried to rape me or anything."

"I wish..."

"Look, Zachary, I like you. I think you're a good teacher. I'm used to you, you're used to me. If I switched to someone else, I'd have to start all over again. And I'm kind of anxious to get this last test over and done with. So, like I said, I'm going to pretend this little incident never happened, okay?"

We're standing by the door. I reach up, put my hand on his cheek for a moment (yeah, yeah, I know; I'm truly evil). Now he's really miserable. He stares at me all forlorn and sad and helpless. I give him my million-dollar smile, then leave.

I am powerful, I am strong, I am in control, I think as I walk towards the bus stop.

So why aren't I enjoying this?

Chapter 14

Suddenly, everyone's leaving. Tasha and Jordan are moving to the newly renovated projects on Mystic Avenue, and Dell's been accepted into the single-room-occupancy housing on Sewell Place, behind Star Market. The vestibule fills with cardboard boxes labeled "Kitchen," "Toys," "Junk." Tasha chooses a powder blue bathroom theme; Dell prefers peach. They comb the circulars from Bradlees and Ames and Caldor's, compare finds, begin most sentences with "This would look nice..." For those of us who are staying, for me, their frenetic activity, their passionate disdain for various decors, is both touching and surprising.

"Oh! I can't stand those geese on everything!" wails the usually dour Dell at breakfast one morning. This switch from cranky to pouty is most definitely welcomed. There's even a hint of playfulness in her sudden concern for matching towels and shower curtains.

Moving day is Saturday. Two yellow rental vans idle outside as we all try to help. Jordan fusses and demands to be held as each of us, struggling with lamps and bedding and clothes on hangers, ignore his uplifted arms and walk around him. Dell curses; Nadine loudly complains at the weight of each and every item she carries; Tasha, in a daze, wanders from room to room, uselessly picking up some tiny thing, then discarding it somewhere else. Rose tries to organize everyone else, resulting in half of Tasha's stuff being put in Dell's van. It is Florence, of course, who steps in and gets the whole thing back on track. By noontime the vans are loaded.

Margaret has made lunch for all of us. In her usual thoughtful way, she has woven each of our favorite dishes into the menu. We hold hands in silent grace for the last time.

"I miss Shannon," says Nadine with her mouth full. It is the first time anyone has mentioned her in a long, long time.

"Yeah," agrees Dell. "I really missed her this morning! Remember her energy? How she use to buzz around the room? She would have had those vans loaded by ten o'clock!"

And for a moment we're together again, all of us.

After lunch there are hugs and goodbyes, tears, and promises to keep in touch. Dell climbs into her truck, Florence climbs into the driver's seat beside Tasha and her son, and they all drive away.

"Guess you'll be next," Nadine says to me as we walk inside. I just shrug my shoulders.

The new woman, who is expected to arrive this afternoon, will occupy Dell's old room. Shannon's old room remains empty. We haven't talked about this. But we seem to agree that there is something vastly, gapingly unfinished about Shannon and this house and that by keeping her room empty, we will be prodded to collectively work on her, her life, her death. Shannon's room is a memorial, a shrine (although Margaret and Florence and Lily and all the other good Quakers would be horrified at such an idea). I know. I sometimes open her door, look inside, smell the still air. Her personal belongings have been removed, of course, but there remain those small reminders, like a snapshot of Tiffany and Justin taped to her mirror, a trace of the scent of her shampoo, that linger and name this space "Shannon's Room."

But Dell's room is ready to become something else. Those of us who remain spend a couple of hours vacuuming, disinfecting, scrubbing woodwork, scraping photos and pictures torn from magazines off walls, preparing the house for our new guest. I work in Dell's room. It is a perfect ceremony for me, a kind of ablution in reverse: instead of a ceremonial cleansing to prepare for the arrival of a loved one, I scrub and dust and scrape Dell from my life.

In the movies, women like Dell and me would come to some kind of understanding just before the credits. But in real life, there are people who hate you and you hate them, and there is nothing going to change that. Dell's broad shoulders and rolling gait repelled me; she looked at me with contempt. After our huge fight, we simply existed beside one another. Sad, really. For Dell and me, living at Esperanza Place was supposed to be a kind of un-numbing experience, a chance to wake up and smell the coffee. But for both of us, the minute the other one walked into the room, all our old little tricks to deny what was in our faces, all the skillful ways we'd developed over the years to not really feel what we were really feeling, or to feel something but to not be able to identify it, just kicked right in. Without effort.

Perhaps, I reflect, as I line the bureau drawers with recycled Christmas wrapping paper, Dell was a kind of a gift, a kind of constant, irritating, and painful reminder of how easily I shut myself off from myself.

The doorbell interrupts my reverie. The new woman has arrived. Quickly, I put the cleaning stuff away and wash my hands. I smell like Murphy's soap. As I make my way downstairs, I can hear Nadine and a strange voice in the kitchen.

"What's this?" the new woman asks, holding a ceramic, lidded jar. It is not so much a question but an accusation.

She's young, no more than twenty, I'd say, with Farrah Fawcett hair feathered away from her acne-scarred face. A sneering acne-scarred face. No makeup, wearing a grey non-namebrand sweat-shirt and sweatpants, she stalks around the kitchen picking things up, putting them down.

"The honey pot," answers Nadine and gives me a look. "Jewell, this is Meredith."

"Call me Scutch. Everyone does. Honey! You got any sugar?" In a few syllables, Scutch has dismissed everything here as perhaps pretentious, perhaps precious, certainly not normal, not what she is accustomed to. Nadine shrugs, points to the sugar canister, and I leave the kitchen.

I knock on Margaret's door. "Can I talk to you?" She gives me a wan smile. "Sure. Come in."

No preliminaries: "This new woman. She's dangerous. I want her out."

"Dangerous?" Margaret drawls the word out; it's either a stalling technique or she's trying to appeal to my sense of irony.

"Dangerous," I say firmly. "She's stomping around the kitchen like she's going to kill someone. It seems our kitchenware is too special for her working class sensibilities. She'll go ballistic on us, I guarantee, and one morning Florence'll come in here to find all of us slaughtered in our beds. Guaranteed."

Margaret seems to be praying. She's quiet for several moments; her focus is clearly inward. "Which approach do you think will be the most effective with you, Jewell? To remind you that a certain someone showed up on our doorstep – filthy, exhausted, hungry – and that another guest urged me to not let her in, either? Or should I remind you that we've both seen this behavior before. This rage – and you're right; she's very scary – isn't exactly new, is it? We both know where it comes from, we both know what it's about. And (now there's an edge to her voice) we both know that over time, wonderful things are possible for Meredith..."

"She calls herself Scutch."

"Scutch?"

"Yeah. It's Italian. I've heard it before. It means like a superbrat. A bitch on wheels. Get the message, Margaret?"

"And I'm asking what message you're getting. Huh?"

"Oh, I get it. 'If you don't like it, why don't you leave?' Is that it, Margaret?"

Now she really looks tired. "You know that's not true."

"I don't know what I know," I yell and leave, slamming the door behind me.

Yes. Slam. Not some timid little slam, either, but a major, teeth-jarring SLAM! A very satisfying thud. The sound, the tension reverberate throughout the house. In fact, the whole house shakes for a moment. These old Victorian houses are strange mixtures of really solid and really flimsy. When a heavy oak door is slammed, the entire house wobbles as if a subway track ran beneath us.

So now everyone's aware of my outburst. Now the others' hearts race – Margaret's, Nadine's, poor, pathetic Rose's. Maybe even Scutch's. Muscles tense.

Good!

I can feel them listening, waiting as I stomp up the stairs. All of us living here share memories of these moments: the slap; the outburst; furniture overturned, glasses smashed; screams; and then, the silence.

In the brief time it takes me to climb the stairs I can feel the entire house relive a shared memory.

Without thinking, I enter Shannon's room. Again, I slam the door as hard as I can; a dust jimmy in the corner leaps up, then settles again on the floor. Violently, I open her window. A shaft of late-afternoon sun reveals more dust. I drag a chair across the bare floor as loudly as possible to stare outside. Shannon's window looks out over our tenderly cared-for garden. In one corner, an ancient rose bush, perhaps planted when this house was new, is in bloom. Its crimson blossoms climb to the top of the recently repaired trellis. Our seedlings flourish. A cardinal trills in the maple tree next door. A tiny white butterfly drifts across the yard.

My heart is not warmed by these things. Indeed, the growing things, so smug, so secure in their carefully constructed plots, mock me. Their possibility sneers at my condition. I could tear them out by their roots!

Those seedlings. So helpless. How easy, how satisfying. it would be to yank them all up, leave them in the sun to shrivel. But the rose bush...

I think about tackling that rose bush, pulling it out of the ground, branch by branch. I think about its thorns, so like a thistle's leaves. I imagine the thorns tearing my bare hands. I think about the extremes of New England seasons that bush has weathered: the hurricanes, the blizzards, the scorching sun, the neglect and foul air it has seen. The rose bush's survival speaks to me:

Endure. Stay in that dark place as long as you must.

And so I stomp back downstairs and without speaking to anyone, grab the vacuum cleaner, noisily bring it and several more loads of cleaning supplies to Shannon's shrine, and I vacuum and I scrub and I wax and I polish. And as I clean I remember. All of it. I play and replay horrible tapes until I am exhausted and the room sparkles.

When I think I am ready, I close the window. Quietly, I return the cleaning supplies to their proper place, again making several trips. On one such trip, just as I am almost to the top of the stairs, I see Scutch scoot out of Nadine's room.

Our eyes lock for a second. My instinct is to turn away, keep on walking, ignore what I've just seen. But since the day I got here, it's been drummed into me what I am supposed to do at a time like this:

"What were you doing in Nadine's room?" I ask, my voice high-pitched, quivery. And I bravely take a step towards her.

"None of your fuckin' business," Scutch snarls. I step back. And we stand silent for a few seconds glaring at each other.

"You gonna tell?" she says finally, her pale eyes pleading, her voice almost a whisper. Tell. Like a kid. For the briefest of time, her little-girl question confuses me. Tell? Tell them? The authorities, the grown-ups, those others? Everyone I offended by my recent behavior? No, of course not! I waver.

"What were you doing in there?" I repeat.

"Nothin'! I swear to God, nothin'!" Her voice rises. I stare hard at her, then turn and go back to my room. But the moment I enter my room I sense something: someone has been here. Nothing is missing, I have nothing worth stealing. It is only when I touch my notebook that it becomes clear what has happened. Someone came into my room and read my stuff.

I open the pages. Yes, she lingered here and here and on this page. I feel her within my pages, hear her slow breathing, her heart beating faster as she reads about herself.

Hello, Loser, I furiously scribble on a blank sheet, I know you were here. I know you read my writing. I'm going to make you wish you never snooped into my personal business. I'm warning you: don't you ever come in here again.

There's a scream from another room "My ring! My ring's gone!" It's Nadine. No question what ring she's talking about. She wears a big opal ring on her left index finger sometimes; it used to be her mother's. Nadine's shrieking as if she's been beaten.

Oh, God, what have I done? Helpless, I stand in front of my mirror and stare at myself. Through my closed door, I can hear Margaret slowly come up the stairs. Now her low, soothing voice duets with Nadine's shrieks, and still I do nothing. Move! But my body remains before the mirror; I can't look at myself now. I close my eyes, and in my mind I see Scutch running down Broadway, I see her at a grubby counter somewhere, I can see her selling Nadine's ring. Do something! As if waking from a drugged sleep, I begin to move towards the door. Picking up speed, I quickly I run downstairs and into the kitchen.

"Is Scutch still here?" I demand.

"Well, yeah, she's setting the table," Rose answers, gesturing towards the dining room with her head. Ha! The fool! "You know, Jewell, I didn't like the way you..." Rose starts in.

"Later. Save it for later." I command. I can hear Nadine and Margaret come downstairs. "Let's eat."

We are a sullen, silent, tense group at dinner. Even Scutch seems subdued. I try staring her down, but she avoids my gaze. Just as Rose fills our iced tea glasses, the doorbell rings. It is with relief that I leave the table, look out the peephole. It's Dell.

"It would be you," she growls as I open the door.

"It would be you!" I counter. "What happened to your face?" By the hanging lamp of the vestibule, I can see her clearly. Her face is a sickish greenish-yellow hue, she's all cut up, her lip is swollen, her right eye blackened.

"I got jumped."

"Where?"

She stares at me, then almost grins and answers slowly, "In my room." Her shoulders slump.

"But..."

"It was Nancy, Jewell." Dell replies patiently. Dell's some-times-girlfriend. "She'd been... oh, hell, think Margaret'll let me stay here a couple of days? I got some sorting out to do."

I study her injuries for a moment. Then I speak. "I'm telling ya, it's never been as bad as it is right now. The new guest? She calls herself Scutch. And she shouldn't even be here. She's real young and has a serious attitude problem. She... ahh, never mind. And Florence has the flu again. And something's wrong with Margaret. Seriously wrong. I think she's very sick or something." I stop. When did I decide that? Then I just shake my head for a moment in disbelief. "Are you sure you want to come back here?

Things generally suck."

But Dell dismisses these domestic crises with a sweep of her hand. "I got no place else to go," she says simply.

We look at each other for a moment, the coats and jackets and boots around us a mute testimony to the peopled and therefore troubled quality of Esperanza Place.

With an ironical heartiness, I usher Dell into the dining room. "Look who's decided to grace us with her presence for a few days," I announce to the surly crowd. "And it just so happens that Shannon's room was cleaned. Today, as a matter of fact. Dell can sleep there." Margaret stares at me; she nods her assent.

Still sniffling over the loss of her ring, Nadine is just passing around heaping plates of strawberry shortcake, our first strawberries of the season. Despite her misery, Nadine has adhered to her usual policy. When it is her turn to cook, food proportions are more than generous. Rose and Scutch, after staring at Dell's battered face, attack their jumbo-sized desserts with obvious pleasure. But the rest of us cannot be mollified by treats; we sit, we chase one strawberry around our plate, we sculpt whipped cream. Yes. Real whipped cream. Nadine greedily eyes our nearly full plates. I know for a fact that later, when she clears the table, she'll eat all our leftover desserts, standing with her back against the refrigerator.

There's a great deal on all our minds as we troop into the library. Nadine sits in her usual spot, the right corner of the couch. She props a box of tissues beside her, then huddles in her corner, tears streaming down her moon face. Rose sits at the opposite end of the couch and stares at the ceiling, the floor, the opposite wall. Scutch, although silent, radiates a deadly rage at us all. Dell sits beside me on the floor. She, too, cries silently.

I watch Margaret. I feel Margaret. As we sit in silence, my breathing patterns hers. So that when the silence is broken and the recriminations and accusations and condemnations fly –"I hate this place!"; "I don't want to name names, but…"; and the ultimate statement: "I don't feel safe here!" – I experience Margaret's deadened response. She is exhausted, she is in pain, she cannot sort all of this out for us.

One by one, the group looks to Margaret. We wait for that wise, calm voice, a few carefully chosen, deeply felt words to make it all better. We wait. "Margaret?" someone says tentatively. She doesn't reply. No such words, no insights are forthcoming. We wait.

After what feels like hours, she finally speaks: "As you have probably already guessed, I haven't been feeling well lately. Shannon's death... well, I don't have to explain. I've talked this over with Lily. As soon as Florence is back on her feet, she'll be taking over and someone will be hired to take her place."

"But you can't..." "What about..." "Couldn't you..." "Have you tried..." In vain we argue with her, try to do as she's so patiently tried to get us to do a hundred times before: brainstorm, explore options, problem-solve. One by one, we come to the same conclusion; it's no use. Margaret is leaving.

So we again lapse into silence. And after a while Margaret speaks. Her words are halting, almost slurred; she uses the wrong word from time to time, with some effort corrects herself.

"There's a story someone at Meeting told of, uh, a wise old man, some kind of spiritual, uh, leader... teacher. From India, I think. He was about to die... no, no, I'm not dying, just tired. Anyway, his followers were feeling, you know, angry, abandoned. And they said something to the effect of 'Don't leave us!' And he said, 'Where would I go?' Not that I am some kind of, you know, sainted person. If I am anything, what I'd like to be is some kind of reminder that there is that of Spirit in everyone. In each of you. So where would I go?"

One two three: "What the hell's that supposed to mean?" Scutch leaps to her feet, grabs a pillow from Nadine, slams it to the floor. "'Where would I go?' she repeats mockingly. "You'd leave. That's where you'd go. They all go. You all leave." She walks toward Margaret. "You shoulda told me you was planning to leave when I interviewed for this place. I never woulda..." Margaret makes some slight conciliatory sound, a kind of back-of-her-throat cooing while at the same time pulls herself into herself ever so slightly, as if braced for a slap.

"Sit down," Dell bellows. "Can't you see you're crowding her?" Scutch remains where she is. Dell jumps up. "I said sit down!" She spits each word.

"Oh, so now I gotta deal with some dyke," Scutch doesn't take her eyes off Margaret but takes a couple of menacing steps toward

Dell. "Maybe you're all dykes!" she accuses wildly. Margaret inhales sharply; that blow hurt.

"Both of you sit," I command. Much to my surprise, they do; there is a palpable relief that someone has a clue as to what to do next. "Thank you. Now, Scutch. Maybe you can tell us something. What were you doing in Nadine's room this afternoon?"

"You're crazy, you know that? I was nowhere near Nadine's room! You're the one started this whole thing with your swearing and slamming doors and shit. Where do you get off asking me..."

"Well, what were you doing?" demands Nadine.

"I wasn't! I swear! The bitch's seein' things. Tryin' to cover her own ass. I swear I wasn't..."

"Let's have some silence for a few minutes. And Scutch, I need to see you in my office when this is over." Margaret bows her head.

"I swear I..."

"Shhh," hisses Dell.

Each woman's presence washes over me as we sit in edgy silence. Yes, washes: like waves, their individual breathing patterns, their smells of shampoo and sweat and laundry soap, break over me like the waves of a secluded harbor. I feel them, us, struggle against one another, or maybe it's against an ever-present offshore wind we're countering, or perhaps it's the inevitable New England rocky coastline we heave ourselves against again and again and again. Our struggle takes on its own rhythm. ONE two three four, ONE two three four, again and again and again until we weary of the struggle and surrender to the rhythm.

My father told me once that every drummer is constantly counting. He said that if you asked a drummer how many steps he just took walking down the street, he'd be able to tell you. I tried it on a drummer I was sleeping with for a while. We were on Amsterdam Avenue between 123rd and 124th on our way to the laundromat. He just looked at me like I was crazy.

I feel Dell, her sadness that she's back here, her anger at Scutch. I feel Scutch seethe; she's in a panic. Is Rose bewildered by it all or guilty? She's a cipher. And Nadine, her face wet with tears, scrunched up over there in her corner. No amount of whipped cream can compensate for the loss of her only prized possession.

Ahhh. A telepathic plot hatches: While Scutch meets with

104

Margaret, Nadine and Dell plan to search her room. And yes, indeed, I see them look at each other, grin. Rose looks up as if she's just caught a few notes of a favorite piece of music. She searches the room expectantly, she smiles, she bows her head again.

Now, as the silence deepens, I stop searching for signs and omens in the faces of these women I live with and move into myself: I see a kind of decaying, rotting, foul-smelling swamp, a pit of unbridled rage and casual cruelty, a cesspool of pettiness and unquestioned vanity. I see it, I smell it, I am sickened by it. I own it. It's mine.

A sigh and then another sigh and then a kind of a gasp. I look over at Margaret. Somehow I know that she, too, contemplates such a place; we stand beside each other at the edge of the slimy water. Margaret? My perfect Margaret? This is her swamp, too? Is this some kind of vast subterranean horror we share?

I'm remembering reading about a man who had drowned in one of those Indian-name lakes in upstate New York, and his body was found a few weeks later in a different Indian-name lake miles and miles away! Folks speculated that those deep, deep lakes, all made at the same time by some glacier, were somehow connected at a depth difficult to imagine.

Margaret smiles at me. Her light fills the room. And yes, I hate her for leaving and yes, I am terrified of what's going to happen next and yes, I am always alone. It all just crashes over me, and I'm awash with tears. I sob. I just break down and cry and cry and cry.

"Don't cry," my mother used to hiss. "It'll spoil your makeup!" Even after I'd stopped modeling she'd say that.

It's Dell who's awkwardly stroking my back. I know it's her without even looking up. Sometime real soon, tonight, maybe, Dell's going to do or say something to piss me off again. But for right now, I am grateful for this momentary truce.

I feel the warmth of her hand, I feel Margaret from the other side of the room, I sense the others' relief at my body-wrenching sobs. Like a violent thunderstorm at the end of a too-hot summer day, my grief cools the charged air. So I just stay in this sorrow. I just wail and wail and wail until there's nothing left.

And finally, exhausted, I am done. The cessation of my tears seems to mark the end of a ceremony none of us quite understands;

we shake hands in a formal, self-conscious way. Everyone quietly leaves the room but not before conveying sympathy toward me with a few pats on the back or a hug or something mumbled. Even Rose and Scutch.

I sit by myself and I wait. For like the aftermath of a thunderstorm, the air is clean, expectant. I wait for what will present itself in this hallowed moment, a time washed clean by my tears. I believe I can smell my rose bush. I watch the evening breeze fan the lacy curtains. I wait.

And when it is made clear what I ought to do, I walk to Margaret's office as if my heart were not beating hard and fast and my body not shaking.

Margaret and Scutch, her face distorted by pain, look up. "Are you allright –"

"Can I use the phone?" I demand. "It's long-distance." The urgency in my voice will not be denied. Wordlessly, Margaret points to the phone, then motions to Scutch for them to both leave the room.

And then I grab the receiver, dial the never-forgotten numbers quickly before my resolve disappears.

"Hello, Mom? It's me. Jewell."

Chapter 15

"How 'bout something like this?" my mother asks, squinting at a dress label. We're shopping for my graduation dress at my favorite used clothing place, The Garment District, in Cambridge. It's a huge, loftlike place, the size of a ballroom, located on the second floor of an old industrial building near Kendall Square. For a decidedly funky place, its wares are beautifully organized by style and color. I appreciate that. Debby Harry's singing over the PA system; a pink-haired, eyebrow-pierced young woman, making her way through the forest of racks, brushes past my mom; a life-sized plastic horse rears on its hind legs just behind her.

But we could be in Filene's for all she notices. She is focused on her mission; we came here to buy me a graduation dress, and you can bet we're not going to go home empty-handed. This is the mother I remember: single-minded, task-oriented, intense. Eagerly she holds out her offering to me. "This peach color would just look stunning with your coloring, Jewell."

It's a suit for chrissakes, it's pastel, it's got tacky gold buttons! Suddenly I'm exhausted. "Well," I say, very drawn out, very carefully, "I was thinking more along these lines." And I show her a '50s crepe sheath, black, sleeveless, with a square neck, and the unmistakable smell of old fabric.

"Why do you wear so much black, Jewell? Is it something the Quakers make you do?" she asks, eyeing the sheath with suspicion.

"They're not a cult, Mom. They're just some people who started a shelter. I can wear whatever I want." As hard as I try, I can't keep the defensive tone out of my voice.

She winces. Again. There are certain words that cannot be spoken between us. One of them is "shelter."

"No," I say, trying again, this time aiming for a conversational tone and failing. "I just like black." The syllables come out harsh and bald and cold. To my mother's ear, my fifteen years above the Mason-Dixon Line have apparently flattened my tone, roughened my speech. Her Southern accent surprises and offends me.

So here we are in my favorite used clothing place, this mysterious person who is my mother and I, and we're once again surrounded by other women's castoffs. "Oh, yeah, huh!" as Shannon used to say. Meaning: Hey! I get it! The used clothing connection, right? But do either of us allude to this shared memory? No.

Since the moment she got off the plane, I have been assaulted by memory. Flooded. Overwhelmed. And very, very confused.

"You're wearing White Shoulders," I had said as we awkwardly hugged, the airport crowd milling around us. "Grandma used to wear that," I had added in what was probably a slightly reproachful tone. My beloved grandmother, my mother had told me on the phone, had died just last year. "I've been wearing White Shoulders for years," she replied crustily as she shook herself free from my embrace. This voice, this tone I remembered as clearly as the scent I was breathing in. But it was the wrong person wearing that perfume! And this tense, little body in my arms? Had she always felt so bony, so taut, so brittle? I'd wanted to hold her a little longer to tease out the memory, try to put the pieces together in my mind. But she wouldn't let me. She stepped even further back from me, fussed at one of her trenchcoat's sleeves as if to erase my touch from her shoulders. "Let me look at you," she had said.

And although I had anticipated this moment, still, I felt myself stiffen. How many times had I been scrutinized by those eyes and found woefully wanting?

Slowly, she took in my hair, wilder than usual in the Boston humidity, the vintage sundress I'd carefully chosen with its old-fashioned, glittery, ruby buttons down the front and cherry blossom print on a pink background, the mauve espadrilles, straw handbag.

"You look like a Renoir painting!" she exclaimed, her eyes wide, lips in a slight smile, and a chill filled my gut. "Let's get your bags," I mumbled.

She, I decided as we made our way to the baggage claim, looked positively feline. Sleek. Pampered. Smug. Absurdly content. My mother has remarried. To money.

"Welcome to Boston," I said to this well-dressed stranger.

It would be a slight understatement to say that my mother's introduction to Esperanza Place was a tad bumpy: her arrival coincided with Scutch's departure. Yes. After much discussion and prayer it was decided that Esperanza Place was not "appropriate" for a scary, nasty, thieving bitch like her. Most of us were real glad to see her backside; Margaret, of course, took Scutch's leaving as yet another failure. So. Just as our cab drove up to the house, there was Scutch, two black garbage bags at her feet, standing on the sidewalk screaming: "Fuck alla yuz. Ya bull dyke! Fuck you!" A white-faced Margaret stood on the steps. A fat, sweaty, middle-aged woman behind the wheel of a beat-up old station wagon kept yelling: "Get in the fuckin' caah," over and over. As my mother and I approached, Florence came outside and threatened to call the cops. Only then did Scutch shove her stuff into the back of the wagon. She climbed into the passenger seat, slammed the door in a final act of defiance, and went off in a black cloud of hot, smelly exhaust.

"You must be Jewell's mother," said Margaret coming down the steps to greet her. "We're delighted to have you." And she stretched out her hand in greeting to my mother. Limply, hesitantly, my mother shook hands. I looked away in embarrassment and disgust. What was wrong with my mother? Why did she shake hands like that? Was it because women don't shake hands in Lynchburg, Virginia; or because she was afraid to touch someone just dubbed a bull dyke?

Rose and I had worked hard to make that evening's meal special: there were fresh flowers on the table, a nice tablecloth, spinach lasagna with Rose's special spaghetti sauce, garlic bread, and a big salad.

"So who was that unpleasant person?" my mother asked as Rose passed her a lemon ice. She'd exhausted her small talk repertoire. How could she have known that her question broke one of Esperanza Place's unwritten rules?

"She used to live here," Nadine replied curtly and shot a meaningful look at Margaret. My mother, not a fool, did not pursue the subject.

After dinner she went outside to smoke, then joined us for evening worship. We were settling down when she came in, smelling like tobacco. Cautiously, she sat down in the rocking chair, then listened as Margaret explained the process. Her jaw set grimly, her arms wrapped tightly around herself as if to ward off blows, it was not clear if she was afraid or disapproving of this silence thing. She watched us, she waited, she rocked, furiously at first, but then, as the group quieted, her rocking motion became more calm.

After about ten minutes, Nadine spoke: "I'm wonderin' if we did the right thing by Scutch." Dell groaned and looked like she was about to say something, but when Margaret shot her a warning glance: Shut up. "No," Nadine continued, her voice raised. "I mean it. I know it was my ring she stole, and I'm glad I got it back. But I mean, maybe we shoulda given her a second chance? We gave Shannon plenty of second chances. Why not her?"

My mother turned to Dell and waited to hear what she had to say. Rose sighed deeply. Dell took her sweet time to speak.

"Here's the difference... well, no," she corrected herself, "there are two differences. First of all, the only person Shannon was dangerous to was herself. But Scutch! She was really scary the way she would just fly off the handle. She pushed my 'Flight or Fight' button bigtime. Who wants to live with someone like that?" She looked around the room for support.

"Not me!" chimed in Rose.

Dell held up her hand to indicate she had more to say. "Shannon had... possibilities. But with Scutch? It seemed like it was too late for her. Stick a fork in her; she was done." She looked at Margaret's sorrowful face. "I know that's cold. But we all know it's true. Even you," pointing to our mentor with her chin. "There are some people who are just beyond hope. And there's nothing we can do, no matter how much we try, to... to... oh, shit, what's the word..." she looked my way.

"Redeem?" I offered.

"Yeah. Redeem them. The second thing is, Scutch came here after Shannon died. So we're a lot more realistic, I think, about our own possibilities. Shit, man, look at me! One week on my own and I come crawlin' back." She looked like she might have more to say but then shook her head in disgust and retreated into herself.

Although Dell hadn't given the most profound message in the world, exactly, she hadn't made any connections that any of us hadn't made for ourselves, I was glad she'd spoken. While she talked, I watched my mother listen as though attending a live performance. And although you can never know how these things affect somebody else, particularly when that somebody is practically a stranger, I was nevertheless grateful my mother and I had shared Dell's "insights" together. I smiled at her. Warily she smiled back.

"I think we need locks for our rooms," Rose burst forth. "In the last shelter I was at, all the rooms had locks. How come this place don't?"

"I guess we thought we didn't need 'em," Florence shot back.

"That's stupid!" replied Rose.

And maybe she was right. All over America that night, folks were buying guns, putting bars on their windows, arming themselves, punching in numbers on their home alarm systems, teaching their children not to talk to strangers. Who were we, in the midst of all that, to live so naively?

But as I was thinking this, I knew I was wrong. So I waited and finally, even though I would have preferred to remain silent in front of my stranger/mother, I spoke: "But what are we saying here? If we put locks on the doors, we're not only saying that we don't trust each other, we're saying that the possibility of trusting each other is dead. Finished. Not happenin'. I wanna live with possibilities," I said heatedly and again tried to catch my mother's eye.

I felt like I'd just given a stellar performance in the school play; I looked into the audience for my beaming mother's standing ovation. I felt like I'd just won the Boston Marathon. I felt...but something – a smell, a word, a memory – had overcome my mother, and she sat slumped in the rocking chair, head bowed, gently rocking herself.

There is a sanctity to these moments when the mystery of another soul is revealed. Who knows what she was thinking? Staring at her unhappy face now somehow aged, I decided she was entitled to feel those things, think those thoughts. Alone.

My mother didn't look up for the remainder of the hour, and after we'd shaken hands, she excused herself and went to bed.

The subsequent two days have revealed something else: the enormity of our estrangement. This gap is so frightening that we have both retreated into a kind of tour guide/tourist role. She exclaims and marvels, I take her by her elbow, steer her around. Sort of. For while I am clearly in charge as we've traveled the Red Line, ridden the swan boats, explored Beacon Hill, there is an intermittent acknowledgment between us that she is the mother and I am the daughter.

"Wipe your chin, Jewell. You've got butter on it," she commanded yesterday as we lunched at an outdoor cafe near Rowe's Wharf. And I automatically reached for my napkin when the acknowledgment of her peremptory tone froze my hand mid-air. I glared at her for a moment. "Well, you do," she said, more gently this time." And then he bought me..." She rattled on and on as I seethed and stared at Boston Harbor.

One of the very few safe subjects between us is her new husband's generosity, his numerous gifts of jewelry, a nail-polish red convertible. She loves to brag, I love these momentary let-ups from my abiding confusion. An old beau from her high school days, Wheeler Taylor had begun courting my mother a few months after his wife Lucy, another high school chum, had died of breast cancer. Always frail, even in high school, Lucy was to discover that married life meant first a series of miscarriages and then an eight-year bout with cancer. "That poor woman was always in the hospital," my mother exclaimed, trying to infuse her tones with compassion but somehow just sounding smug. In six short weeks, my mother and Wheeler had married, honeymooned in Venice, and bought a house on Peakland Place two blocks from my grandparents' house. Wheeler sells real estate. Wheeler clearly adores my mother.

Earlier today, while my mother cheerfully vacuumed the dining room, I'd gone running into Margaret's office. "Why in the world did I call her?" I wailed.

"You called her because when you sat quietly you had what is known as 'a leading,' Jewell," Margaret had explained to me. "You acted on what you discerned was the right thing to do. However," she added, staring at my distraught face, "it's always a good idea to sound out other people about a leading. Check it out with someone else. Sometimes what we think is something divinely inspired is actually too much caffeine or our own ego or just some random thought. These things can be dangerous."

"Why didn't you stop me?"

"You were pretty determined, as I recall."

"Yeah, well I'm not now."

"So the visit isn't going well?" she asked carefully.

"Nothing's real, nothing's said. We're tiptoeing around each other like... I don't know." I stared at my hands for a while. "The only question she's asked me so far is how Shannon died." Margaret simply sat quietly. She looked at me with those wonderful, deep, caring eyes. We listened to the vacuum cleaner being dragged across the floor.

"I wish you were my mother," I said.

"None of us gets to choose our parents," she said wearily.

I jumped up. "I know that! Tell me something I don't know, will you? Like what the fuck's going to happen to me? Huh? I'm thirty years old, I'm just now getting my fucking GED, I have no skills, no clues, no nothing. I've got an idiot for a mother! And you're leaving. Thanks a lot, Margaret. Thanks for nothing." And once again I stormed out of her office, slamming the door as loudly and emphatically as I did the first time.

I heard the vacuum cleaner being shut off and my mother following behind me as I stomped up the stairs.

"Let's go shopping," she said to my retreating back.

My mother studies the dress. And I study my mother. I see a fifty-year-old woman, artfully coiffed and dressed, signs of impending middle age showing around her carefully made-up eyes, the hint of jowls. She brightens. "I saw something like that…"

"Mom," I say with sudden urgency, "I have something to tell you." And I practically drag her over to a store area done up to look like half a subway car. "I Want to Be Sedated" blares. She sits on the long plastic bench, crosses her legs at her ankles, folds her hands on her lap, fearfully looks at me. "What is it, Jewell?"

And I tell her. I tell her about Mr. Allen. I tell her about the disastrous reunion with my father. I tell her how I've survived all these years. I point to the mock subway car we're sitting in: "Before I came to Esperanza Place, this was my home for a couple of nights." And as her dark eyes ever widen and then fill with tears as I go on and on, my question is answered. What did my mother know? Not a damned thing.

Calmly I get up, walk over to the place where they sell used tablecloths and napkins and such, and bring back an old-fashioned flowered handkerchief with purple lace trim to her. ""Don't worry," I say as she looks at me questioningly, her makeup all messed up. "I'll pay for it." She blows her nose into the multicolored fabric.

And thank you, God, she doesn't tell me I'm a goddamned liar. Thank you, Spirit, she doesn't tell me I somehow "asked" for all of this to happen, she doesn't blame me or tell me it's my fault. She doesn't wonder what I did to encourage all of this, she doesn't discuss some fatal flaw handed down from generation to generation. All of which, as I have heard from the others, being distinct possibilities. No. By some miracle, this stranger/mother does just the right thing: she holds me close, strokes my hair, tells me how sorry she is. She believes me.

Her hairsprayed hair is rough against my face. I want to push her away, but there is something about her physical presence I need to know: Ah, yes, there it is. How frail she feels. How tiny. My Amazon mother has shrunk into this little person who is wearing White Shoulders. Like her mother used to.

"I miss grandma," I say.

"So do I." We hold each for a few moments and then, suddenly, she pulls away. My mother jumps up, agitated. "That little

113

worm," she says, furious. "That snake! He's gone, you know. Moved to Chattanooga. But I'm going to find him. I'm going to track that man down. He must be stopped. They keep doing it, you know. They just move from one family to the next. I saw this thing on Oprah…"

Suddenly she puts her hand over her mouth. I watch as my mother realizes that some horror she saw on Oprah is a living, breathing reality for her daughter. I watch my mother take her first tentative strokes. Now she's swimming in it, too. Well, no, not swimming, really. Not yet. Treading water's more like it.

Much as I had wondered (No! Let's be honest, here; obsessed is a better word) about this conversation, there are no claps of thunder at the revelation between us. The heavens have not opened wide. No angels sing. An ugly little secret has finally been told. Truth sits here between us as palpable as the clothes and the scents nearby. Yet I feel no lifting of my spirits nor am I suddenly transformed by my mother's knowledge. And while perhaps in my most clear, most grown-up, mature moments I never really expected everything in my life to suddenly change, get better, for the pain to somehow – Poof! – vanish, I am surprised and saddened by how unhappy I do feel. For I realize that in a few days my mother will return to her comfortable life back home, her complacency now forever cemented by the belief that all those lonely, bewildering years she spent wondering and worrying about me were the result of my dark secret. We will never, she and I, talk about our shared life before Mr. Allen. We'll never discuss, as they say on the GED, "the underlying reasons." Underlying. Lies underneath. Truths not spoken. The price I pay to know what my mother knew is that we will forever remain strangers.

I do not understand how I know these things; I only know that I see relief in her eyes. She is off the hook. I see something else there, as well: Pity. In her eyes, I shall forever remain a victim.

Chapter 16

SCALE graduation night is garbage night on Broadway. Our group: Margaret, Florence, Dell, my mother, Rose, Nadine, Tanya, me, and Jordan in his stroller walk past some truly odiferous trash cans and plastic bags, many already torn and scattered by marauding dogs and cats. In contrast, Somerville's numerous rose bushes in full bloom spread their perfume. There's a metaphor to these feuding scents, I suspect. Were I not so preoccupied by this evening's impending event, I might be pondering their essential (or at least what I can come up with at the time) meaning.

I am walking with a pretty glum crowd. Dell's still with us and shows no signs of leaving. Tasha's looking worn out; life on the outside doesn't seem to agree with her. Someone called her a nigger the other day as she was hanging up her wash on the community clothesline. Welcome to the projects, Tasha. We're all worried about Margaret's imminent departure and the fact that Florence seems really spacy these days isn't exactly helping matters any. And like the time when Shannon died, I can feel the resentment from the others that I'm getting all this attention. "What's the big fucking deal?" I heard Dell say as she and Nadine were loading the dishwasher. "She passed some tests. So what!" Yeah, these are not happy campers. Except Rose. She smirks and smiles, keeps giving me these knowing looks. Is this the way she shows jealousy? Or is she just demented?

"I still can't get over this city," my mother is saying for the umpteenth time. "Everything is so spread out but it's a city." She teeters along on perilous heels. We tried to warn her that our route meant climbing both Winter and Central Hills, but she archly reminded all of us that Lynchburg was also built on seven hills and that her outfit "required these particular shoes."

She's wearing a powder blue linen suit, knee length, and chunky 14-carat gold accessories. She wears matching blue eye shadow on her lids and carries a white clutch bag, which matches her white pumps.

My Garment District chemise has been duded up with gigantic rhinestone earrings and black hose textured with roses. When she saw the entire ensemble, she pronounced me fit to be seen in public. Thanks, Mom.

We're walking past Louie's ice cream stand. Cars are double parked on Broadway, and the brightly painted picnic tables are filled. "Isn't this nice!" my mother gushes.

"It is," Margaret agrees. "We thought we'd come here after the

115

ceremony."

"Won't that be nice!" My mother chirps.

Talk about contrasts! Watching my mother and Margaret together, who are essentially the same age, certainly the same generation, has been, well, confusing. For all their differences in style and manner, they both possess a kind of civility peculiar to their generation and class which masks their differences. Both of them – Fading Southern Belle and Aging Hippie – have the ability to be polite, to rely on form and manners in a way I cannot. Nor do I ever want to.

By the time we cross the bridge over the railroad tracks on School Street, we're all huffing and puffing. "Why didn't we rent a limo?" Dell half-seriously demands.

And, indeed, purring like some kind of gigantic mechanical feline is a gleaming white stretch limo parked in front of Somerville High. When a grinning twentysomething in a shiny cerise prom dress steps out of the back seat and waves her champagne glass to the crowd gathered by the front steps, I want to turn back. Flee.

"I don't think I can do this," I whisper to Margaret.

But then Zachary emerges from the crowd milling outside the school and, very shyly, hands me a bouquet of flowers.

"These are for you. I wasn't sure you'd come," he says.

"Who's this, Jewell?" my mother pushes past Margaret and stares at the now-blushing math tutor. For a moment I see him through her eyes: gawky, scrawny, slump-shouldered, unimpressive. And he is all of those things. But I see something else; I know he understands my embarrassment at hard it was for me to pass that test. I know he understands that the simple-for-some-people computations on the GED math test were, for me, an enormous obstacle. I know he understands how hard I had to work. I see respect in his deep-set eyes.

"This is my friend… my math teacher, Mom. Zachary." I pronounce his name with the reverence, the significance it deserves. And I flash a million-dollar smile his way.

"Very pleased to meet you," she replies convincingly.

"Let's go inside," someone urges. We mount the stairs and walk into the cavelike auditorium. The stage is brightly lit, its azure-blue curtain almost iridescent under the stage lights, but the

116

auditorium seats remain in partial darkness. I am directed to a table in the middle of the central aisle. An aide from the testing center, now wearing her Sunday best and a corsage, takes my name, gives me a number on a little slip of paper, and shows me where to sit.

"There was someone looking for you," she reports.

"Zachary?"

"No. An older man… there he is, over there." She points.

Standing on the side of the auditorium is my Dad.

He sees me, comes toward me. As he approaches, he sees my mother in the group behind me. Something like annoyance briefly registers on his face but he keeps coming toward me. He gives me a bear hug; we speak into each other's shoulders.

"How did you…"

"Someone called. I had a hell of a time finding this place…"

"But who…"

"Hey, kid, I wouldn't of missed this… you look great, kid."

"Mom…" I say warningly. He pulls away then, walks over to her, says something none of us can hear. She hisses something back.

He gives me an over-the-shoulder look of complicity: Do you see? Can you understand? Do you blame me for leaving her? I look to Margaret. She shakes her head.

"I'll see you after," he says. "I want to hear all about your plans." And he heads up the aisle.

What plans? Lately, all I seem to be able to do when I am alone is cry. What plans?

"We'll be over here." Dell directs the group, my group, including Zachary, to a very different part of the auditorium.

"But I thought it would be a good idea," I hear Rose wail. Of course. Rose. Only Rose would be wily enough to locate my father, stupid enough to think I'd appreciate such a gesture.

Unseen by any of them, I slip outside. The early evening sky is far brighter than the auditorium; I stumble almost drunkenly to the little park between the high school and the library. There's an empty bench near the swings. A young man heartily pushes a little girl. Her features are delicate, her fine, brown hair pulled into a topknot. Like Shannon used to wear. He's wearing a white tee shirt which partially covers a large tattoo on his left biceps, jeans. A cigarette dangles from his mouth. The little girl must be about three, maybe younger; it's hard to tell because she seems small for her age. She can't quite make up her mind if he's pushing her too hard or not. She's staring intently into his face as if he might have the answer. He might be able to tell her how she's feeling.

My parents.

"None of us gets to choose our parents." Margaret had said. Apparently I don't even get to choose when one of them reappears in my life.

And then Margaret sits down beside me.

"Why did he have to show up? I don't want him here!" I wail. The man and child at the swing stare at me; I lower my voice. "I mean, it's bad enough that I'm thirty years old and just now getting my GED. But to have my mommy and daddy here? It's a mockery, it makes me feel really, really stupid!" I turn to her. "Why would he think this would be a good idea? He's an idiot; they both are." And I start to cry.

"So, technically, they're your parents. So what? All of us can be parented by lots of different people. I think we all can get what we need from whomever is able to give it to us. Look at the group that..."

"Yeah? And what happens when you leave?"

"I don't know what's going to happen. But I do know this: You have to ask, Jewell. You have to pray. You have to figure out what you want, what you need, and then you have to ask for it."

"But what about all those people Hitler killed? They prayed, didn't they? Where was God for them?"

"I can't answer that question. No one can. All I can do is affirm who I see right before my eyes. I see you, Jewell. No one will ever get on the cover of "Time" for getting her GED. No one ever wins any awards or prizes for walking away from abusive relationships or stopping drinking or anything. You're one of our success stories, Jewell. And I can tell you how glad I am you came knocking at our door."

The little girl squeals. She's decided she's having fun. And although I'd thought I'd outgrown my belief in omens and augury, her laughter seems like a sign that I'm supposed to go back inside. I'm supposed to attend my high school graduation.

"What did I miss?" I ask as I sit back down.

"Nothing. Boring stuff from the members of the school committee," says the woman next to me. "This guy's a stand-in for the mayor," she explains. A well-fed, suited man drones on and on. Gradually, after focusing on my quick-beating heart, do I register something: children. Scattered throughout this large darkened space are, from the sound of it, hundreds of babies and children of all ages. Their young voices create an almost-shrill pitch, certainly an agitated, insistent noise, which at first I find extremely annoying. I mean, couldn't these people find babysitters? But then, looking into the faces of the women surrounding me (and most of the graduates are women) as they fan their faces with their programs, I understand.

And indeed, as the evening progresses and the student speeches are given, speeches by the graduates of the various programs SCALE offers, a central and underlining theme is established. Every person graduating here tonight (and from the looks of the program, there are hundreds of us) is connected, somehow, to an army of supporters and well-wishers: neighbors and babysitters and family members who picked up the slack so a mother could study, children who ate haphazard meals at haphazard hours, saintlike partners of every sex, race, and age who, as was gratefully noted again and again by the speakers, were "there for me."

"Wait," says the woman who's been sitting next to me as we line up at the foot of the stage. She speaks with a heavy accent. I think she's Greek. "You look like a raccoon." And she gently wipes under my eyes where my mascara had run.

"Thanks, Mom," I say.

Forgive and let go, the AA folks say. It's a goal, maybe. Something I could shoot for. Maybe. I hear a swell of voices. I hear Dell and Nadine and Tasha and Rose and Zachary. I hear my mother and my father and ladylike Margaret whoop and shout and scream and whistle as my name is called and I walk across the stage to receive my certificate.